The Hag at the Neck

Geoffrey Phillips

CHAPTER One

Beginning

I'm sitting on one of the comfortable rocks looking out at a group of terns flitting over the water in loose formation. I love their distinctive chirps — so much sweeter than the harsh cawing of the seagulls. The small waves lap at the stones near my feet, and swirl in their gurgling way across the shells, seaweed, barnacles, crabs, and into the spaces among the rocks, where the level seems to rise and fall as if the rocks themselves were breathing. As the tide comes in and then recedes, I will sit different places, and the patterns and noises of the waves will change. There's a light mid-August breeze that blows a few hairs down across my eye. I brush them back into place. A small sloop is passing about a mile offshore, beyond the island. I inhale that rich scent of salt and sea air.

It's 4:00 pm. Getting up is always a bit painful until I'm

vertical. Stepping over a few of the larger chunks of granite, I step on scrubby sand and broken shells, sprinkled with occasional tufts of sea grass and lavender. Over the past year, I've lined the path from here to the house with stones and shells that at one time or other struck my fancy. When a major storm comes through it wipes out my little path. The treasures that edge it, that I've carefully selected over the past few years, are gone. I can never find any of them again. But week by week, I spot new ones, and rebuild the walkway.

My cottage is really an old fisherman's shack. Someone later added the kitchen and dining room to it on the east side, closer to the water. In the back, I have a bedroom, storage, and utility closet. That's it. Early on I made a sign for the cottage out of driftwood. 'Bleak Point' seemed to appropriately capture the feeling of this place and the feelings inside of me at the time.

When out on the rocks where I'd been a few moments ago, looking at the terns, I experience moments that aren't bleak at all; but facing inland to the west, it is, to be honest, pretty dismal. For it's impossible to look at my cottage, coming up to it from the water, without also seeing what's behind it, toward the road; and that is a fish-parts processing plant called J&M Products. The air is sweet now, as the breeze is coming in from offshore. At other times, I'm treated with odors from the plant — the very smells that keep visitors away and that enabled me to buy this cottage so cheaply.

Thinking about that now brings back a sort of ironic memory. When I was nine, I spent a summer at some relatives in the Carolinas. They lived near a quarry where all the local kids went swimming when it was warm enough.

That was back before it was boarded up. My brother and I would climb up to the rim and jump — sailing through the air, gathering speed, until we crashed into the water. It took a while to get the technique right so that you didn't belly flop or get your nose crammed full of water. It was all idyllic except for one thing. My relatives and the quarry were located near a paper pulp mill — where my uncle worked. As you approached the town, as I did that summer, you couldn't miss the stench of pulp manufacture. On arrival it was awful. By the third day, you didn't really smell it anymore. I mean, you could smell it, since it was there, but it wasn't annoying. It was just sort of hanging in the background. When vacation was over, I remember getting on the bus back out of town. As we traveled farther and farther away, you could sense that the smell wasn't there anymore — the air, coming in through the open bus window, was crisp and fresher. But when we changed busses in Richmond, there I was, feeling all fresh, and yet everyone who came near me moved away or held their nose. I couldn't smell anything unusual. And it continued right till I got home. My mom said, "Hi, honey. God, you stink. Let's get you and your clothes washed."

So, as it was with the pulp mill, it is with J&M. I don't really mind the odors any more. They're just there in the background. I only notice them now when the wind is blowing easterly from the plant across my cottage, when the plant is really busy, and when the air is heavy. At those times you almost feel the odor as a physical thing, like a massive flow of sour molasses, oozing out of J&M, across the junky space in between and then, slowly enveloping my entire world.

The little plot of flat land around the cottage is a mixture of sand, crushed shells, and occasional rocks. At the beginning I tried to get a garden growing outside the dining room window. I thought herbs might be nice, and bought some basil and thyme. I was pretty sure they wouldn't grow in the sandy, salty, shell-infused mixture that nature provided, so I lined up some stones into a little wall next to the house and bought some potting soil. I'd also read somewhere that the Native Americans used to put a fish in the soil as fertilizer when they planted corn. I didn't know if it would work for herbs. To be honest, I didn't even know if the story was true. But living where I do, it was no problem getting a bucket of fish remains, which I spread around under the soil. I was diligent about watering, but so was nature. A week after I'd planted everything, the rains came and the angle of my roof line turned out to be such that a torrent of water streamed down on my little bed of crops. The next day, everything was gone. All that remained was a wet ditch.

When I was seventeen I was in love with Sally Richmond. She was blond and a bit on the tall side. I was shorter, but in some perverted way, that made it work. She had what I always called a sparkling personality, and it blossomed when she was looking slightly downward at me.

That may have been the last time I was really in love — back then, as a kid, when I didn't even know what love was. We did all the teenage fondlings, but mostly enjoyed being with each other. We could be serious together and help each other with homework, but we could also have fun — she more than me, since when it came to fun it always turned out that I was more of a participant than an instigator.

I remember Sally sitting on a table in the cafeteria, cross-legged, and pretending to be Mr. Pfoxon. Mr. Pfoxon was a guidance counselor who was paralyzed from the waist down. He had a mustache, and there was Sally, finger across her upper lip, bouncing around on her butt on the table, doing a perfect imitation of the Pfoxon drawl.

A month later, and I would never again think there was anything funny at all about someone disabled.

It was the spring dance — not a prom, but a big deal. I had my license then, but no car. Sally had a license and car, so she drove. None of us had any alcohol that night as I remember it, but coming home from the dance on Lantern Road, Sally was probably driving a little fast, and decided to tell a joke that I can't recall that seemed to require that she stand up and sit down while driving. I was looking right at her — right at her ecstatic smile and laugh — as the car missed the turn and swiped the tree.

When you're recuperating, you don't really have the distance with which to objectively assess what has really happened to you and how your life has changed. So for the first six weeks it was mostly just words. "You were really lucky." "A miracle they could save the eye." "If your arm had been hanging out the window, you would have lost it." "No permanent internal injuries." "I think we've got the leg fixed up pretty well."

Oh, it all sounded just wonderful to be so lucky. And there was more. As it turned out, Sally hadn't been injured at all. She stopped in a few times to see me while I was mending, but her eyes wandered, and her smile seemed short and forced. By the time I could get out of bed on my own, I was informed that my left leg was now two inches shorter than the right one, "but it was a miracle they could save it at all."

I didn't return to school until the following year, and by then I knew full well what I faced and would face for the rest of my life. The piece of window that had "miraculously missed my eye" deeply slashed my face from the bridge of my nose down across the edge of my mouth. It left a permanent, visible scar across my face, and, when it healed caused my mouth to droop down at the left edge. Any time I wasn't careful, drool would leak out and drip down onto my chin. My short leg meant that I could no longer effectively run, and walked just the way you've seen other cripples walk. I was stared at, at first, ignored for a while as other students didn't know how to look at me or what to say. Occasionally I would catch sight of some jerk pretending to walk the way I did, and I'd hear the little circle around him laugh.

Sally Richmond never left my heart, but she moved on to more normal prey. I would think about her often back then, and I still do sometimes, even now, after all those years. I try to hate her for what she did to me, but when her image comes up in my mind, it's the laughing, free girl that I was in love with. I try to hate her for avoiding me when I returned to school, but back then, I felt guilty about the way I looked. I didn't want to look at me either.

I was accepted by Yale, based, I'm sure, on the great essay I wrote about the accident and the change in my life. It was written as a sympathy-builder, but ending with a sense of hope and future. I look around me and see others who have missing limbs or are partially blind, or perhaps just paralyzed. I sense that they've figured out how to regain some center and balance. For some reason, I couldn't. I was the one who was different; I was the one who was always stared at. I did poorly, barely making a C average. English professors who had seen my college essay had high hopes for me, but were disappointed and puzzled by what I wrote subsequently. I didn't seem to be able to step back and gain any sort of perspective from which to write. I didn't seem to have any new ideas. My writing was mechanical. In the nick of time I shifted my major to Art History.

My brother, Arnold, is two years younger than me. When we were kids at school, we were pretty competitive; at least that's what my parents used to tell me. I didn't feel competitive at all. It's just that I was older and as every situation came along, every new thing to try, I did it first, and being older I did it better than he did. At least that's how I like to think of it. But it's also true that every new thing he discovered and wanted to do, I tried to do too, and I'm sure I took a lot of fun out of his life.

Nevertheless, we stayed friends in a brotherly way most of the time and went exploring together, swimming together, sledding together. I don't think we ever got into a physical fight. As we grew and developed our different personalities, we were apparently both smart enough to do well in school. I was forced to learn a musical instrument and chose the clarinet, which I never liked and never played again after age twelve. He learned piano and guitar and still plays them. He developed a sociability early on that I was envious of.

Somehow he could slide into a group — whether it be adults or other kids — and be interesting and engaging. For me, the social world has always been a struggle. It was bad enough before seventeen, and so much of a nightmare since, that I don't even try anymore.

Arnold went to Harvard, graduated with good grades and went on to law school at BU. After a couple of early jobs that weren't quite right, he connected with Bridges and Hughes in Boston. He's now their top public property lawyer and has many of the Massachusetts towns as clients.

It may be that he would have sailed ahead of me anyway, but we'll never know. He certainly kept racing ahead when I was seventeen, even as I was lying in a hospital bed with something inside my soul dying.

I think about poems occasionally and tried to build one up from the line:

He passed the bar while I got the scar

But I was just feeling bitter. It wasn't fair.

While Arnold was in law school I was still in my first job. I was out in the world with a Fine Arts degree, which meant that I wasn't trained to do anything really useful — at least that's the way it seemed in job interviews. I now had three disabilities: the scar and drool, the crooked walk, and the useless degree. When I applied for work at museums, it generally ended up that the public-facing jobs were unavailable. It was due to the scar, drool and limp. No one ever said so, but that was clearly it. And that led to the next problem. In smaller museums, even the good jobs in the back — curatorial, restoration, acquisitions, all overlapped with jobs where you had to present yourself and come across as an engaging person.

I finally got work with a major auction house as assistant to their authentication and appraisal expert. It was a job. So to add interest, I started writing short pieces about art. But once I made the mistake of following up an article with a lecture. I had practiced speaking so as not to scowl and drool, but when the moment came, I couldn't pull it off. The rustling crowd politely sat through the lecture and then hurried out without asking any questions.

The job didn't last forever. At some point a new face appeared and everyone assured me that the newcomer was just there to study or learn or whatever. It didn't matter what they said. I could tell. And six month later it was explained to me that I was reorganized out. 'Nothing to do with your work, John. Your work is great. It's just that with the budget crunch we had to make compromises.' This was followed by the smiling, firm handshake. 'And don't worry. We'll write excellent references for you.'

I don't know why, but the first person I called was my brother. I never cry, but was on the edge of tears. Was this to be my life? To carry around these deformities and never be able to settle into anything? Arnold was amazing. There were times that I thought that he thought I was some sort of simpleton due to the drooling. But he really did an amazing job. The next thing I knew was that I had permanent ongoing disability payments from both the government and the auction house.

These were regular monthly checks, and although not enough to support the life I suppose I'd hoped for, it was enough to live on if I supplemented it with occasional part-time work; and if I wasn't too greedy about what I spent the money on.

Which is all to explain why I live where I do, and why I drive a twelve-year-old Toyota.

It's another day and cloudier, but still hot, even at six am. The water is never like glass, but is close to it this morning. A flock of geese woke me up. I went out and banged a large spoon on a pot to scare them. It's less effective all the time.

When I push off in the small skiff on quiet days, I like to do it gently and watch the vee design flow out behind my boat and across the water. Rowing is my exercise, and since it's all arms, it's pleasurable. I can fully use the parts of my body that weren't destroyed.

On a calm day like this, it will take half an hour to row out to the island. On the way, I survey the receding shoreline. And to my mind, every mariner notices this effect. When you're ashore or near shore or even looking at a top down map or satellite image of the shore, you're struck by how irregular the coastline is. Points, coves, bays, necks, little islets. The shore is anything but a straight line. And yet, as I row out toward the island, the shore line seems, with every stroke, to collapse a bit further into the appearance of a straight line near the horizon.

One minute, I'm launching myself from the middle prong of an E, surrounded by two longer points of land. But soon, they become less prominent and I see worlds beyond the E. I once even had a notion of a poem with that line or title.

Lands beyond the E
Pulling, gliding, firm and free
No longer trapped within the E
Seeing lands beyond what's known
Seeing all, but seen alone.

The idea was something like that. The notion that you can escape from the E to step out and look back at it and beyond, but the price is that you do it alone. It was a dumb idea. No one but me would even know what an E was; and maybe no one but me would think it had to be escaped alone.

But it can't be denied that there is an incredible collapsing of geometry as you move farther and farther out from shore. From my vantage now, out near the little island, I look back. Haddock Point, to the south, is but a smudge. Its three houses are all collapsed together. And the point to the north is dwarfed by Osbourne Scrap & Iron's heap of metal. It is barely possible to see that there is a broken down and abandoned house in front of the scrap heap, visible from here, but otherwise largely hidden.

The gentle scraping noise tells me I'm coming upon the island. Its official name is Merrant Island. I never bothered to find out who Merrant is or was, but he or she certainly didn't appear in any of my history books. I think the locals call it Gull Island in honor of all the gulls who nest there in the spring. All I know is that it's aptly nicknamed, for as I pull in, I'm confronted with the screeching of a thousand gulls. I open my backpack and pull out the broken crusts of bread I've brought. The gulls expect it and come dangerously close, fighting for position. I fling crumb after crumb out for the taking, and watch the birds fight for the next bite. I may decide to stop doing this. I'm beginning to think that gulls are too competitive, nasty and insistent to deserve this sort of generosity.

Maybe that means my bitterness and anger are abating, since part of the joy I've had in watching the gulls having to fight for each scrap is the realization that my life is not quite that bad.

I'm usually surprised when my cellphone rings, since it happens so infrequently. Other than robocalls or crank calls it's usually Angie or Arnold or one of the editors at publications I occasionally write for.

"Hey Jay, it's Arnold."

"Hey, how are you,. How are Marsha and Chris," I reply.

"They're great. They are. We all are. Thought I'd drop by again, Friday. Say 'hi' before my dinner meeting."

"That's nice of you," I said, meaning it. "You've come by a lot lately. It's been nice."

"Always good to see my big brother," he said.

"Right," I said, knowing that he obviously had a business reason for the trips.

"But tell me, Jay. What's new with you. I hear no news."

"I'm surviving OK," I replied. "Between the disability

income, the framing jobs and some writing — those articles on art I told you about."

"Not for me to lecture you," he said. "But you need a plan. You can't just continue day after day, just getting by, can you?"

"I'm fine, Arnold. I really am. I'll be good to see you Friday." I hung up.

Arnold and I have done that dance. His usual word is 'arcs.' "Life is superimposed arcs," he likes to say. "Each one takes you to a new place. The arc of childhood, the arc of education, the arc of love and marriage, the arcs of jobs and careers, of hobbies (maybe those are many concurrent arcs). Don't you see, Jay? Each one has a goal or expectation. Along the way, you experience challenge, curiosity, thrill, or whatever. But it's the arcs that make life worth living."

That's his view. My experience was different. Try to build an arc around a freakish scar and drool on the head of a cripple and you get wobbly lines that aren't arcs at all and that peter out and die, rather than becoming beautiful rainbows taking you to pots of gold. The best I can do is to manage the arcs that have become circles, since they avoid the unpleasantness. The circles I travel are the cycle of the day, the cycle of various odd jobs.

I have a recurring dream that makes no sense to me. I'm in an airport and I'm hurrying to make a flight. But I don't know what gate to go to. There's a display with flight information that I see up ahead. I get on one of those moving sidewalks to get closer so I can read it. But for some reason, the faster I try to hobble, the farther away it's getting. I'm going backwards. People start to pass me, and one little boy turns and says "Your feet are too heavy." I look down and I'm wearing big clumpy shoes. I see now that the people who are passing me are flying in the air. Occasionally someone calls out, "Hurry up." It's clear to me — crystal clear — that if I could get the shoes off, I would fly too. There are clasps holding them that I had buckled that morning, but I can't remember in which order to open them. There are several versions of this dream, but they all relate in same way to my clumpy feet slowing me down in a crisis.

I'm not a psychologist, but I've naturally tried to figure out whether it means anything. I come up empty every time. The easy answer is it's just some deep wish to not be a cripple, and that if I could just do something to fix my legs then I might be able to get to some destination, some place I'm longing to be. Or maybe an acknowledgment that I'm not getting anywhere, that I'm not following any of the arcs that Arnold keeps wishing on me.

When I was young, Arnold and I would occasionally compare dreams in the morning. Back then my dreams often had a heroic aspect to them. I would be leading an army, or rescuing someone, or discovering some treasure. The dreams had arcs. That was all before the accident. Back then, Arnold's dreams were never as exciting as mine, and I know it bothered him. I recall that his worst one was being stuck in an elevator, which then opened on a strange floor. When he exited, he was surrounded by mechanical toys. All moving. The toys weren't doing anything in particular, but they were moving. And the terrifying thing to Arnold was that they were all looking at him.

I think about all this, since today things seem totally reversed. I don't feel much like a hero, and as far as I can tell, there is nothing 'stuck' about Arnold's life.

CHAPTER Two

The Point

As far as I can figure out, this cottage that I rent must be about fifty years old. It's been minimally maintained — just enough to fix leaks, keep the plumbing working and electricity on. The shingling is now a mix of different colors and ages — some painted, and some just plain cedar. The newest part of the cottage is the roof, which finally got replaced last year. In the same way that you get used to the fish plant smells over time, your home — no matter how dilapidated — becomes normal and expected, so that I never find anything unusual in the mixture of shingling that covers the walls, and am never bothered by the fact that the floorboards creak and sag in the dining room, or that the rug is worn thin and the colors have faded to various shades of brown and gray. Besides, when you live in a place like this, your focus tends to be outside.

My dining room has windows that look east and out to sea, and south, down along the shore. I don't spend much time in the dining room, since I have few visitors and generally eat in the kitchen. But if I look south out the window, or if I stand outside where I tried to garden I have a nice view along the shore down to the next point of land. I think of south as the genteel direction. Along the shore, there's a consignment shop, just far enough away from J&M to avoid the smell, then a small diner, and then farther along a cheap motel with canoe rentals. No one ever rents any canoes as far as I can tell.

Farther on, I finally see a house on the shore with a small dock. It's empty from October through April, so I have assumed either that it's just a summer cottage with no heat or that the owners are those clever sorts who have homes in Florida that they occupy six months and one day in order to deprive the local community of tax revenues. Each year when they show up, the two kids look a bit taller, though my ability to measure things from this distance is limited. They have a little Sunfish, and once or twice we've sailed past each other, and waved. I doubt if they saw my face.

Further along, just before the Haddock Point juts out, there's a sandy area where there are a few swimmers in the summer. I can see three very nice houses on the point itself. I know nothing of who might live there — only that the houses are nice and that they define the southern limit of what I can see from Bleak Point. It would be a long row to Haddock Point, and while I've sailed down to it offshore, I've never bothered to try to find a place to land.

I spend a lot of time in my kitchen. It's comfortable there; and in the winter, my wood-burning stove is close by. In the summer, it's on the cool side of the house with one side facing north, the other to the water, which is generally where the breezes come from. I don't know much about weather, except that in the summer, the air which lies atop the ocean and is cooled by it gets sucked toward the hotter places over the land, creating a sea breeze. Apparently it has to do with temperature and pressure.

My kitchen has windows that look both ways. The window to the north is pretty uninteresting. It looks across a cluttered back-property of J&M, which I assume is where they dump everything they don't need anymore. Up along the shore — maybe a half mile north – I can see the Osbourne scrap heap, and the pleasant view of old cars, refrigerators, engine blocks — things like that. Given the high value of waterfront property, it is astounding that what would otherwise be prime real estate is given over to a junk yard. But that's the fact.

I assume they occasionally sell or use some of the scrap, but on the other hand the pile seems to grow each year. I rarely see anyone working there though. Instead I see the mechanical arm of a crane rising from behind the pile, grabbing or dropping something, and then disappearing again.

As I said, I think about how valuable that property might be if put to other use, especially since the land doesn't stop at the edge of the scrap pile, but continues out to what would usually be a picturesque point of land with some large boulders on it. I get a partial glimpse of a dilapidated house there — one side caving in — which would make a prime location, except for the junk pile and except for the rock pile that lies between the house and the water. I assume that at some time, those rocks were intended as the base of a pier, or foundation for a new house to replace the old one. Who knows?

My freshman year at Yale, I read *The Great Gatsby*. At the time I loved it. I loved Fitzgerald's immediacy, and the pace with which the story just sort of unfolded and sucked you in. Nick, the young bond trader, and his infatuation with Jordan. But mostly the wealthy and mysterious Gatsby. The light, visible across the sound from East Egg. And then, even at Gatsby's house, he is, in a way, somewhere else — not part of the party.

I can't remember all the silly ideas that I probably took away from that book as a still impressionable college freshman. Somehow, even though the story ends badly for Gatsby, the book conveyed this sense of the American dream, in which Nick or even I could end up in East Egg, with someone like Jordan.

It only took three more years. By senior year, it had finally been beaten into me that I wasn't the handsome Nick Carraway. That I was the disfigured cripple with the drooling frown that scared the Jordans away. There are so many memories of short encounters, and so many different ways I was rejected and turned down. I'd gotten the message from Yale that my writing was not very imaginative. And so it was patently obvious that the whole idea of the American dream was a fraud — that it wasn't available to everyone, but only a select few. I assume blacks have known that for years. That's their problem. I was consumed with my own. I was an outsider. I was shunned. And I remember taking my copy of Gatsby and actually burning it. I graduated hating that book and hating Sally Richmond, and hating life.

Some things change with time. All those feelings of anger and hate, experienced by a youth still freshly pumped full of hormones and unrealizable desires have faded over the years. What remains are smoldering embers. The feelings never went away, but they no longer consume me.

I suppose that's why I was able to think of Gatsby again when I ended up here. It wasn't exactly the same, of course. The shoreline here was like the letter E, and I wasn't looking across Long Island Sound. I was on the middle prong of the E and looked out past an island to the ocean. But there were these other prongs, to the north and south. And my first summer here, there was a boat tied to a dock at Haddock Point. It was nighttime, and for some reason the boat had its running lights on. The angle of the dock and the motion of the waves must have been caused what I finally saw. It was a flashing green light — the starboard running light appearing to turn on and off as the boat shifted slightly. Gatsby came to mind. The point to the north, with the pile of scrap metal on it became North Egg in my mind — the poor egg; and Haddock Point to the south with the beach and expensive houses became South Egg — the expensive one.

For a month earlier this summer, I stared down at South Egg every night, looking for some flashing light — some sign that there might be an amazing party going on that I could slip into — in the dark, of course, with my face hidden and my crippled hobble unseen. I never once saw a party going on, or a yard laced with glowing, colored lights; and by the end of July, I'd concluded that South Egg must be a depressing place.

Looking the other way, it was clear that North Egg was even more depressing and would never have any wealthy parties, with lights, fountains of champagne, carefree flappers, or music. It was cold, dark and dismal. The scrap heaps were ugly, foreign, cold; and the old house that I could barely see part of, was equally cold, dark, uninhabited.

I do have a car. It's an old Toyota with rust spots. You don't see as much rust on cars anymore, but I don't care. Rust on a car seems consistent with drool from the chin. I decide not to drive the mile into town. It'll take me 45 minutes to walk, but I walk slowly — by necessity — so even in the heat it won't be too bad.

I walk into Angie's Art. The AC is running and it's almost a shock to be blasted with cold air. There's no AC at Bleak Point. Angie is fighting a Pyrrhic battle. She has that critical eye, and takes paintings and small sculptures of regional artists, mostly on consignment. Her problem is location — the key word in retail. She's too close to the industrial end of town — which is also the poor end. There's at least one other cripple here, who hobbles around. More of the blacks live here. The nearby houses are more run down. The local market does a big business in food stamps. You get the idea.

But for some reason Angie hangs in here.

"Hey, John," she calls to me as I come in. Take a look at what I just found."

"I'll sit," I said. "Walked today. But you can whet my appetite. What's new?"

"Two paintings from that woman you met last week. You know how I secretly groan when someone brings in yet another picture of the lighthouse, or of a shell, or of one or two sloops racing across the bay? Well she's done something different. They're sea scenes but painted from a low angle, as if seen by a shell, lying on the beach. There's lots of perspective, and they're well executed. She has a confident technique."

"Do they need frames?" I ask. That's what I do here. I frame things occasionally.

"Sorry. They came in with simple frames, and that's how she wants them shown."

"Well, I'll take a look anyway," I said, rising.

She watched me while I took a look. Did I see a little frown on her face? Is she hoping I'd just go back to the back room where I'm invisible? Is she afraid I'll drive away customers? Or am I making it all up?

The paintings are well executed and they do present the seaside in a slightly different way. But for me it was as if a good commercial artist had simply said, 'Hmmm. Maybe I'll try the same scenes from a different angle.' Angie seemed more positive about them, and thinking through her eyes I could see why. The people who come here to buy are, for the most part, not art aficionados, but tourists seeking things to bring back home – token memories of their visit. They should sell well. The crude frames were a bit gimmicky, but so was the perspective idea.

"How's business this summer," I asked as I walked back toward the door.

"Slow. I'm wondering if I should add painting classes."

"I think everything's slow this year," I said.

On my way back home, I pick up the odors from J&M at about the halfway point. A large crane is doing something up the road at Osbourne's scrap yard. I think about walking up to watch, but my legs are hurting.

At night, when it's hot, I like to grab a beer and sit out on the rocks, watching boats pass, far offshore, their green, red, and white lights seeming to glide effortlessly and silently along the dark horizon. If it's clear, I watch the stars, although it's never really totally black up there — too many nearby lights. Down toward South Egg, lights appear in some of the houses when they're occupied, but it's too far away to get a sense of what's going on; and although I have some binoculars, something in me resists being so voyeuristic.

Behind my house, and up the road at North Egg, security lights remain on, illuminating a still and dead world. And out on the North Egg point, away from the security lights, it's just motionless and dark. I think about it. But for the scrap yard and the generally depressing surroundings, North Egg would be a great place to live. And apparently someone did at some time. But the old house has clearly been vacant for decades. It is largely shielded from my view by the boulders, but I've rowed my skiff past the point and found the place depressing even in the daytime.

There are two boulders in particular that fascinate me. It seems that one of the Osbourne security lights has just enough brightness so that the little sliver of the old house that I see between the boulders is a shade lighter than the black rocks themselves, and the shapes of the facing rocks creates what looks like the silhouette of a tall woman. In the day, when the sun is up and the lights are off, you can't see it, but on dark, clear nights, the image of the woman returns.

I'm watching now, and while clearly the image is motionless, your eyes sometimes play tricks and she will seem to shift, and then you laugh at yourself

Nine o'clock. Time to go in. I'll need to get ready for my brother's visit in a few days. I start to turn away, but then snap back. Was it my imagination? For a second the woman between the rocks seemed to black out, and swivel and then return to normal. Absurd? But I was sure I saw it. I don't know whether to laugh at myself or not. The boulders must weigh many tons; and one thing for sure: they aren't moving.

I go back inside, but for the next half hour, before bed, I take occasional trips outside just to look to be sure. The lady is there. Quite motionless.

CHAPTER Three

Meeting

It's a particularly hot day. I'm wearing just a tee shirt and shorts. It's a green tee that has an ad for scotch on the back, which is interesting since I don't drink it. I don't even remember where I got it. I'm also wearing old sneakers since I don't know what the footing is like on North Egg. It's been so hot lately, and I've been barefoot so long, the sneakers feel strange and confining. Walking down to the skiff I have a premonition and glance quickly up to North Egg. But it is just sitting there as it always is, dark and dismal. The jumble of rocks at the water's edge; the broken seawall; and inland, Osbourne Scrap & Iron's mountains of metal. From the rocks by the water, next to my skiff, I can barely even see the top of the roof of the old house, hidden behind the boulders.

I push off across a few feet of crushed shells. Even that little bit of activity brings out sweat on my forehead and pain in my legs. But stepping into the shallow water alongside, I'm immediately soothed and cooled. My shorter leg goes in first and then the rest of me. I sit there, quiet, just floating for a minute. Many small boat owners experience this, I hear. The activity and scraping and noise of pushing off, and then, for a moment, the absolute solitude of floating, powerless, soundless. Today, the oppressive heat has apparently discouraged the terns and gulls. The heavy air, mixed no doubt with whiffs from J&M is not totally clear, and I can only see a mile or so in any direction before whatever lies behind becomes hidden. The slight haze makes Merrant Island turn into a shadow, and North Egg look particularly unwelcoming.

Clunk. When I first lift an oar, the silence is broken. And in a few more moments everything is moving in the familiar rhythm that I love. The squeak of the left oarlock every five seconds. The soft pwsish sound as the oars enter the water, and visually, the dozens of interlacing circles that form as water drips from the oars; ribbons of the slight wake, the trail of bubbles streaming behind. Even in the heat, the exercise feels good; a rich and growing ache in the shoulders, and no pains from the legs.

Halfway to North Egg, I can look inland between J&M and the junk yard and out toward the road. There's a fenced in area there with nothing on it but tall grass. I have no idea who owns it. I don't see much traffic going by. Perhaps the heat keeps everyone inside. Pull. Glide. My little cottage grows smaller and flatter, and hazier.

I turn and coast, scoping out a place to land. Rocks, rocks,

rocks. I'm near the broken seawall but don't see a good spot to bring the skiff in and go ashore. There's no natural harbor here, just rocks. I just drift, not even sure anymore if I want to go ashore or not. It's quiet again, but then something is moving. I turn sharply and watch two rats scampering around the rocks and then disappearing.

I lean back a bit, straightening my back, elbows on the thwarts, looking at the sky. At the hot sun. I close my eyes and rock in the silence.

"You can tie up at the ring on the old seawall."

For a fraction of a second I fantasized that the rats were talking since I'd seen no other sign of life. I turned, and there, standing next to the seawall was what could only be described as an apparition. The lady in the rocks. It wore a gray caftan, which covered it up to its neck. Its head sprouted straggly, gray hair that fell down around its face and chest. Its hands were hanging down, and seemed delicate; something told me this was a woman. By the time I'd looked back up to study her face, she'd turned and begun to walk back up across the rocks — surprisingly gracefully. It wasn't the lady in the rocks. This was a real woman.

I was now in a quandary. I hadn't planned on finding anyone here. I had simply set out to look at the boulders and the run down house, hidden behind the scrap yard. I was still floating a few yards offshore and could easily turn and row back home. Yet I couldn't. 'You can tie up at the ring on the old seawall' had been an invitation, and it would be rude to just leave, wouldn't it? On the other hand, she hadn't stayed to chat. She'd just left, my presence of no consequence to her one way or another. It was as if she had seen me wondering how to come ashore, had decided to tell me how, and had then gone back to her own life, caring not at all whether I stayed or went. So much of my life had been that way. Confrontations. And then the next moment, after someone notices my disability and dis-figuration, when they suddenly seek to find a way to retreat back into their own world, and build up that insulating space which so often lies between people. But I couldn't leave. As repulsive as this person looked at first glance, and as much as I wanted to leave, I couldn't.

I skulled backwards to the seawall and found the ring down at the waterline on the far side. It turned out that there was also a crude stairway here. It hadn't been built as stairs, but when the seawall fell apart, the stones themselves had improvised. I was really sweating now. Even though it was late, the sun continued to burn through the sky and air. I tied up and pulled myself out onto the rocks.

I looked to the south. My own cottage lay there looking small and inadequate. By the time I'd taken three steps up across the rocks, larger boulders hid the cottage from view. There was no sight of the woman. All I now saw was the terribly run-down house, backed by the scrap piles. The house was dark, though not uninviting. The door was open and I walked toward it, strangely drawn by something more than curiosity.

I entered, and the contrast to the bright though hazy day outside was so great I could see nothing inside. Perhaps she wasn't even here. I wiped my arm across my mouth and chin.

When I sweat a lot, the sweat from my forehead has the embarrassing desire to roll down to my nose, and then down the groove of the scar on my face, and then, perhaps collecting a little drool at the corner of my mouth, drop onto my shirt. I wiped my dampened hand on my shorts. It was even hotter inside than it had been outside.

"Do you want to take your clothes off?" came a voice. I turned and could now begin to see her, standing there next to the far wall.

That threw me for a second, but I replied, "Why would I want to take my clothes off?"

She shrugged and just stood there looking at me, saying nothing. As my eyes continued to adjust, I could now begin to see her facial features. Bushy, untrimmed eyebrows, dark eyes, no scar on the face, but wrinkles. A nose that might have been broken years ago. I looked at her mouth. How do you describe a mouth? It was friendly.

The longer she stood there, the stranger I felt. Her question had thrown me off. I'd parried with a question back — an old trick. But it hadn't led to conversation. She was staring at me almost as if to say, 'No matter.' And I began to feel strangely ridiculous. My answer had been, 'Why would I want to take my clothes off?' What a dumb thing to say! They're my clothes and my body. Why would I be asking someone I'd never met before why I might want to take them off. It was a stupid response. A knee-jerk response; the way I've responded to so many things. And I've always gotten by with it. But she just dismissed my response, obviously knowing it was just a stupid throw away thing to say — to shift the question away from me.

She walked past me, still not talking, and stood in the center of the open door, her back to me, a light breeze entering the house slightly ruffling her disheveled hair. All I could see against the bright sea beyond was a silhouette. She stood a bit to one side and I couldn't tell if that was meant as an invitation for me to stand next to her, but I chose to stay where I was.

I just watched her; and she, apparently uninterested in me, just stared into the sky across the water, her hair blowing in the breeze. She brought her hands up to her neck, and a moment later the caftan had fallen to the floor around her. And there she was. Naked, in the breeze, obviously relishing the cooling air now hitting her entire body, while I stayed back in the dark inside, clothed, suffocating in the heat, sweat in my arm pits and sweat running down my scar.

What should I do? I could just stand there like an idiot, sweating away, or I could storm out, brushing past her, hobble to my boat and row away. But I did neither of those. I unzipped the shorts and let them fall, and yanked the tee shirt off. I wasn't actually naked. I still had underwear on, and I took two steps toward the open door. Oh what the hell. This whole things was so weird, what the hell. I slipped out of my underpants, and walked up to door, standing beside her in the breeze.

Neither of us spoke. Neither of us looked at the other. We stood, relishing the caress of that light breeze across our bodies. I have no true sense of how long we stood there. All I can say is that it was the strangest thing. It was intensely personal and yet totally impersonal. I was in a direct, pleasant, personal communication with nature itself; and at the same time it was incredibly shared. Like some magic spell. It ended when she turned and walked inside, ignoring the caftan on the floor. I turned and followed. She walked across the room to a cupboard, again seemingly oblivious of my naked presence and her own. For me, while I watched, fascinated, it was another moment of decision. The obvious thing to do would be to slip my clothes back on while she was occupied; but somehow that felt as if it would be rude and confrontational. It was easier to remain as I was.

I was self-conscious. There was a small table. I pulled out a chair and sat. She was still at the cupboard, seemingly mixing something. When she had apparently finished, she picked up some objects and turned and said, "Come."

I stood up. She walked back to the door through which we'd entered and out in to the declining day. Now, not in the doorway, but out on the rocks. The sun bright on her naked back and wrinkled, sagging buttocks. She walked over to a flat rock that she obviously used as a table and place the items there.

I was standing in the doorway.

"What are you doing?" she asked.

"What? You mean standing here?" I said, quickly.

She was now facing me in the bright sun. Deflated breasts; skinny and wrinkled; and when she spoke, I could now see that she had a number of missing teeth. She was ugly, and I had involuntarily turned away as I replied.

She didn't say anything, and when I looked back at her, there was a rueful sadness in her eyes. What was I doing? That was her question. I was standing there; but what I was doing was continuing to drift. I'd answered a question with another automatic question. Why do I do that? And what's worse was that after years of growing anger and bitterness at the way my own disfigurement caused others to look away, I, myself had looked away when I confronted what was abnormal. What am I doing? Ironically, that was the right question, for as I thought about it, I didn't like the answers I was giving myself.

I turned back and looked at her, seeing her now as a person and not as another disfigurement. I walked toward her. She picked up a bottle and poured some of its oily contents onto her hand. She rubbed the oil across her cheeks and neck and shoulders. She then picked up a curved stick.

"Have you seen a strigil before?" she asked.

Finally a question that I wouldn't answer with another question. "No."

She said no more and proceeded to use it to scrape away the oil. I was close enough that I could see every detail. The slow, soft scraping of the strigil across her skin, temporarily indenting it and smoothing out the wrinkles. I could see the line of oil that it collected, presumably along with dried sweat and pieces of dirt or dead skin. She would shake the strigil sharply to clean it and then move to another area. The odor was pleasant and intoxicating. The cleaned skin glistened.

Her eyes occasionally wandered around, and at other times stared directly at mine. She examined me, without apparent concern or expression. She cleaned her breasts and stomach and legs, all with practiced motions. I was so captivated that it was a minute or so before I actually looked around to see whether we were visible to anyone else. Here I was standing naked, next to an ugly witch! But there was no sight line to anything threatening; and as I stood there, I began to feel that it didn't make any difference anyway. The whole thing was so bizarre that if someone had seen it, they would have shaken their heads and assumed they were fantasizing.

"Would you do my back?" she asked.

Suddenly a sort of surreal, abstract, dazing experience had become direct and personal. Would I do her back. She hadn't asked it with any emotion attached, so I couldn't tell if it was a question or a request, or a simple 'this is what you do next. Do it.'

But her hands were held out to me — one with the oil, one with the strigil. I took them. She turned her back to me. I almost panicked for a moment. Here I'd been watching her do it for the last few minutes, and suddenly it was my turn. How much oil? How long to rub it in? How hard to scrape? How large an area at a time? I poured some oil into my left hand and started rubbing her left shoulder. It felt warm and soft. It made me want to keep rubbing. But finally I took the strigil and with parallel, vertical strokes produced the look of glistening skin I'd seen her achieve earlier. I wasn't as quick as she was, but I decided I'd done pretty well — only feeling really nervous while doing her buttocks.

She turned and for the first time smiled, showing her missing and crooked teeth. "And you?"

I swallowed and nodded, not knowing quite what to expect.

She had me turn slightly. The most surprising thing about the next few minutes wasn't the experience of the strigil — though that was pleasurable enough — but it was that, for the first time, rather than throwing out ambiguous questions, she talked — or rather, she led us through a conversation, albeit a short one.

She poured oil across my shoulders, put the jar down, and began to massage them with both hands.

"I asked you what you were doing, and you didn't answer," she said.

I wasn't going to fall into answering with a question. So I said, "I'm trying to survive. Isn't that what everyone does?"

Shit, I realized. I've done it again. A question with a question.

"You are trying to survive," she said.

"The sun comes up. I go about my day. That's what I'm doing. Is that what you want to hear?"

She suddenly went expressionless in that way of hers. I could tell she was thinking, by the increased pressure. But she wasn't speaking. And I, of course, was recognizing that I'd done it even one more time. Another stupid question.

She cleaned my face and my chest.

"You are trying to survive," she said.

"OK. I am. I live in that dump on the next point. I have

trouble keeping jobs."

She looked at me with a soft kindness and said nothing. It wasn't until she was doing my legs that I realized that as opposed to everyone I'd encountered over the past dozens of years, it was this strange, ugly women who had never taken a second look at the scar on my face; who had expertly oiled and scraped it clean; who was doing my legs with no concern that one might be shorter than the other.

I was overcome by something different. I looked right into her eyes with something akin to hope. I wanted to say many things — and very different things than 'I have trouble keeping jobs.' I wanted to say that I don't know who I am. I wanted to say that I'm terribly unhappy — deep down — even though I hide it. I wanted to say...

"Turn around," she said, kindly.

I did so, and she did my back. Standing there on a point of land, looking at the ocean, viewing miles of vista and not just a nearby wall. Standing naked and having oils rubbed caringly into my back, and then the gentle strigil scraping them off I felt released in some way. I felt, for the first time in decades that there might be other possibilities, or at least approaches to life that had been invisible to me before.

I started to speak. "I..."

But her mouth came up from behind to my ear. "Shhh. Relax. Feel the moment. Listen to the breeze."

And I closed my eyes, standing there, totally naked, next to an equally naked ugly old woman.

I did. I listened. I relaxed.

Later I followed her inside and went through that period of adjustment to the darkness after being in the sun. I felt clean and refreshed. I liked the way I smelled, and for a few moments, I even lost track of the fact that I was still naked.

"I have lunch ready for us," she said.

Another surprise. How could she have lunch ready when we'd just been outside for the past many minutes?

"You didn't even know I was coming," I said. There! Not a question.

She just smiled, and so I couldn't help myself. "OK. You say you have lunch ready. Do you always have lunch ready? Was there some reason you expected me to come here?"

I paused and then added. "Those aren't dumb questions in response to your questions. I really want to know."

She continued to walk around behind a counter, putting something together. "You use words without thinking. You assert what I know or don't know, when it's information not accessible to you. You use the word 'always' in a way that forces me to say that no, I don't always have lunch ready. And then strangely you ask not whether I expected you to come, but whether there was a reason behind it. Your words are walls. They wall you in. They're defensive. That tells me you're not free inside."

I didn't know what to say to that; and my lack of response didn't bother her in the least. At some point, two plates were complete, and she carried them to the table. She sat. I sat across from her. We looked at each other.

"Fine," I said. "Did you expect me today?"

"I knew you'd come," she replied. And right there in that moment I was again struck by a difference between this ugly woman and other people. Everyone else I'd ever met who caught you in a gotcha, made a facial expression when they let you know — a sort of I'm better than you look. It's often just an instant, but it's always there. This woman had nothing like that on her face. She was simply telling me that she knew I'd come. It wasn't said as if it was remarkable; it was just stated, and then she picked up her fork.

I picked up mine. "What's your name?" I asked.

She put her fork down and looked at me. "Why did you ask me that?" she said.

Now she was replying with a question, but there was an earnest, pained expression on her face as if the question were somehow of vital importance.

"I'd like to know what to call you, while we're talking," I said. "It makes conversation simpler. I'm John, by the way."

Her face totally relaxed. "Call me Hester," she said. That was another strange comment. She hadn't said her name was Hester, just that I could call her that. A mystery for later.

Time for me to be a polite guest. "Thanks for the meal, Hester."

We ate. It was unfamiliar food, but tasty. But I was still burning with curiosity. When Hester had been busying around finalizing our meal, she hadn't set the table. It had already been set for two.

"I don't see how you knew I'd come here," I said. "No one could have known, but me."

"But you see? You did come. As I expected."

"You'd have to be able to see the future. Can you do that?"

She took a forkful of food and chewed it slowly. "Can you?" she asked. "After all, you knew you'd come."

"But that's different..." I said.

"Why did you come here?" she asked.

"I was curious," I said.

"About what?"

"About what was here."

She looked at me again with deep, soft eyes. What was she thinking? What was I saying? It seemed that everything I said to this woman was some sort of meaningless empty statement. She'd called it defensive, and I guess it was, although what I was defending wasn't clear to me, or why it was worth defending.

She spoke. "You're thinking about meaning. Aren't you." It wasn't even a question.

Hester nodded in a strange way and got up.

"There's a little privy on the south side of the house. I'll be a moment to the north."

I went out to the little shed and relieved myself. I was increasingly wondering what I was doing here, and why I was still naked without it bothering me. Why had I come here? I could have rowed down to the beach, or even to Haddock

Point, or maybe even out to Merrant Island, though the currents might make it a challenge. But I had come here. Today. And she had expected me. What did it mean?

I walked back inside, once again feeling blinded for a moment. She returned at about the same time.

She looked at me as if willing some communication, and walked across the room and through a door leading toward the back of the house. I followed her into a large room. There were two north-facing windows which brought in a modest amount of light. The walls were covered with paintings. She stood by, silently, while I walked around and looked at them.

"These are quite good," I said. And I meant it. I had studied art and wrote about it; and, if she were the painter, she had real talent.

She hadn't replied, so I looked at her, and saw that distant, slightly sad look of hers. Was she thinking of some lost opportunities? No. She was once again quietly observing that I'd made another meaningless statement. The paintings were good, but I could now sense that she knew it and wasn't seeking confirmation. I opened my mouth to speak again, and realized I had nothing to say.

"How do you define art?" she asked.

My field. I cleared my throat. "Let's see. Art, and I assume you mean fine art, is the creation of objects that are visually appealing, or which evoke a positive response in some other way."

She stared at me. She walked over to a long counter and

unscrewed a container.

"Lie down," she said.

"Where?" I asked, not seeing anything suitable to lie on.

"On the large canvass on the floor."

Wondering what would happen next, I complied.

"Lie on your side, but as if you are carrying a pumpkin and running."

I actually laughed at that, but I rolled to my side and tried to comply with the strange request. She didn't speak, and approached from behind, but soon she was moving around me, brush in hand, painting the outline of my body onto the canvas with blue paint. It was done with practiced care, but yet she didn't seem to mind that occasionally the paint would streak along an arm or leg as well as the canvass.

When she was done, she stood. I sat up and watched her go to the counter. In a moment she was back with another brush and can.

"Your turn," she said.

I got up, and she lay down flat on her back, shook her hair and then repositioned her arms and legs with only a slight turn to the side. Her straggly hair was flung out in all directions from her head. She looked carefree and stared at the ceiling with an expression of almost ecstasy. For an instant the old, shrunken hag was transformed into a carefree girl. It was stunning and almost made me wonder if she had some magic way to make that happen.

I knelt down, and with less practiced motions, painted her

outline. It was atop mine, and so, whether I got a little of the red paint I was using on her or not, she would clearly rise with blue paint all over her back. She obviously cared not at all; and she didn't say a word when I slopped paint on her hair. I didn't know how else to paint the outline, and for some reason didn't want to ask. She apparently didn't mind.

When I was done painting, she stood, looked down at the canvas, nodded and said, "Let's get cleaned up. It's water based.

I had seen no sign of running water or electricity in this old house, and so was curious about what she had in mind. But it was soon clear. She grabbed a towel and walked back through the front room and out the door. She dropped the towel on the flat rock, walked across crooked stones and dove into the ocean. There was apparently something to stand on, since in a moment she was upright in chest-high water, running fingers through her wet hair and then rubbing her hands all over her body.

"You'll need to do my back," she said.

I hobbled across the stones and dove in. I found the rock to stand on, and washed her back. She checked mine. With her wet hair plastered to her head she looked less like a witch.

"Have you found meaning yet?" she asked.

We dried off and stood, naked outside the house.

"I should probably go," I said. I didn't want to go, but didn't know what else to say. The whole experience had been so strange. I knew nothing of this woman other than that she was carefree and insightful. She was ugly and maybe that's why she hadn't seemed to notice my deformities. No, that wasn't it. It wouldn't have mattered what she looked like, she wouldn't have noticed them anyway. They were irrelevant to her, to what was going on in her head, and her life. She was seeing me, being with me, in a different way.

I wanted her to plead with me to stay a while longer, but she shrugged and walked into the house. I stood there for a moment wondering if there were something I should say, but once again I couldn't think of anything. I walked into the house. I couldn't see any sign of Hester — if that were her name — so she must have gone into one of the back rooms. There were two doors, one to the room where her art studio was. I had no idea what was through the other door. I thought about opening it. What if I did, and she was there? What would she say? 'Curiosity again?' or maybe 'I knew you would come.' More likely she'd say, 'I thought you were leaving.'

I found my clothes and dressed. I walked out of the house, across the rocks to the broken seawall. I had a fleeting thought that with the change in the tides, the skiff might be grounded, and I'd have a reason to go back. But it wasn't grounded. Its stern was in the water; it's bow about a foot in the air, supported by the line tied to the ring. With the weight of the skiff pulling on it, it took a few minutes to untie the knot, but I did; and even in the lower tide, the rocks still made an easy stairway down to the boat.

Pulling away I could see that this point of land, North Egg, was pinched into a sort of neck where the house was located. From my cottage, it had all looked like a continuous jumble of strap metal, large boulders, and a hidden old house, but from here it was evident that the house was separated from the scrap and that the point fanned out a bit near its end. The very large boulders had probably been left by a glacier, the smaller ones pushed onto the point to expand the scrap area. No consideration had been given to the house, since it was falling down anyway.

As I rowed, I thought about the strange day. How could I do otherwise? I thought about how alive I'd felt — even in my confusion about what was going on. I thought about all of that I still wanted to know and find out. Who was this Hester? Why was she there? Did she really know I was coming? And then I stopped. I even stopped rowing when I realized that if the day and the conversation had gone down those normal, predictable paths, it would have been just another day, meeting just another person with just another personal history. Somehow the day had become electric because it didn't do that. It was all immediate. No interest in where you were, who you were, why you have a scar on your face. Live the moment.

I shrugged and started rowing again. I didn't know what I was talking about, but there was something important going on. I thought about my lame answer to the question, 'how do you define art.' I had rolled out s string of words. Just words, no thought behind them. So in a sense, I'd said nothing. And she responded accordingly by saying nothing.

And then there was that last question that was still hanging in the air, floating along beside me as I rowed. 'Have you found meaning yet?' For some reason that draws me back to memories of standing in the door and feeling the soft, cooling breeze; and then being oiled and scraped with the strigil.

'Listen to the breeze. Feel the moment.'

What I actually feel is the skiff scraping the near rocks as I arrive home to Bleak Point

CHAPTER Four

Return

The next morning I awoke feeling refreshed and alive. I had gone to bed early and slept well. I gave long thought to just climbing in the skiff and rowing back over to North Egg , but realized I had a short article I needed to get out today. My cellphone rang. It was Angie. A hurry-up framing job had come in. Could I pretty-please get over to the store and do the job? I'd get double the normal fee. I agreed and then set out to plan the day. Three hours should be enough for the framing, and I needed about the same amount of time for the article; but then I'd email it, maybe have a follow-up call; and maybe there'd be a glitch with the frame.

I regretfully decided I couldn't go back to North Egg today, and that, due to the uncertainty over how difficult it would be, I'd better do the framing first. I drove the mile to Angie's instead of walking. Angie explained the project and had already selected the frame style and matting color. The picture was large and it took me half an hour to set it to the backing so that it wouldn't wrinkle.

As I worked I occasionally thought about North Egg and about Hester, and I found myself whistling (Yes, despite my scar and lip, I can whistle). When I was finished, I sprayglued a label on the back. I walked back up to the front of the store and handed the picture to Angie.

She glanced at me instead of the picture and said, "You must be happy with the job. A bit of sparkle I haven't seen before."

"I…" I didn't know what to say, so I said, "Thanks. I think I'm happy with it." But my happiness had been from thoughts of Hester, and standing naked in the breeze, and lying on canvas painting ourselves. I left the store still whistling.

Back in my cottage, I completed the article. It took a little more research than I'd thought it would, and so it was already five o'clock when I finished. It would be almost insulting to row over to North Egg now. It would be like saying, 'I'm back, but you weren't the important thing today. But here I am. What new surprises do you have? Gimme, gimme.'

I cooked and ate dinner. I'd go to North Egg tomorrow. It would be the important thing I do. And first, I'd make a stop at the market and have them fix up some picnic salads.

I sat outside again that evening, looking at the stars, but mostly glancing over to the large boulders and the woman between them, eternally frozen into stillness.

When I'd visited North Egg two days ago, I'd departed around seven pm at near low tide. It was now two days later, low tide would be closer to nine, and high tide around three. So, leaving at noon would give me a full six hours of higher water which would assure my skiff didn't end up dangling from the painter.

As I shoved off with the bag of lunch salads between my feet I realized I had no reason to expect anything. She might be gone, or she might greet me again, standing on the rocks in the gray caftan. I began to row. If I kept that old mooring pole lined up with the center house on South Egg, it should be a perfect line to North Egg. I rowed and rowed. There were other possibilities, of course. She might be standing outside, stark naked, with some other person scraping her down with the strigil. She might have five or six people over for lunch — although it still wasn't clear to me how anyone would get to that house from the street.

Strangely, none of those thoughts made me nervous. Perhaps I felt a bit of entitlement. This was *my* witch that I was going to visit; and maybe somehow she would again know that I was coming. She might even know I was bringing a picnic.

I began to sweat as I rowed. Sweat stains growing on my shirt at the arms and chest; beads running down the scar, mixing with drool and falling from my chin. I tried to recall if I had gone anywhere at all in the last twenty years when I hadn't been self-conscious about my appearance. That thought caused me to suck in an extra-large breath, and call out, 'yes!' to the terns.

I was rowing faster. I wanted to be back on North Egg with Hester, the ugly witch about whom I knew almost nothing. But that wasn't true. I knew she was a free spirit; I knew she was a good artist; I knew I felt something totally new and refreshing just being with her.

I wasn't paying attention, and slammed the skiff right into the sea wall. I whipped my head around to see if I'd been observed, but the point looked quiet and empty. I tied up the skiff, leaving a little extra line, just in case, and climbed toward the house, carrying lunch. No sign of anyone. The door was open, as it had been through my entire visit the other day.

"Hello?" I called into the dark room. There was no reply. I walked in, waiting for my eyes to adjust. I had a fleeting thought that I might see a body on the floor, but there was no body, no one else. I looked at the table wondering if through her strange magic, she'd known I'd come, and had left something to eat. There was no food on the table.

There was however a note. I walked over to read it. 'John, Come back tomorrow.'

I put the lunch bag down and felt deflated. A little rivulet of sweat and drool ran off my chin and fell on the paper. The ink started to bleed. I watched it, fascinated as if there were somehow another message in this. But if there was, I never found it. The handwriting was neat, without flourish. But, assuming that Hester was elderly, the note displayed no shakiness at all in the penmanship. I read the note again — silly since it's only four words — but looking one more time to see if it had begun 'Dear John,' or if it had ended with some meaningful sign-off and then her name. But neither of those was there. Maybe she was simply telling me that since I didn't come back yesterday, she'd be gone today. But I couldn't make that work.

I walked toward the door and looked out, dripping sweat. A light breeze was coming in, and that made up my mind. I pulled my shirt and shorts off and just stood, naked in the doorway. I tried to get thoughts of Hester out of my mind and just experience the breeze. But I did keep thinking of her and wondering if she would materialize behind me, also naked, and then, wordlessly stand beside me, the only sounds being the gulls and turns and lapping waves; all in harmony with the whispering breeze and our breathing.

I must have stayed there twenty minutes or so. In the end, no one showed up. I skipped the strigil, though I thought about it, got dressed, and walked back down to the skiff.

The rowing back was heavy. I tried to get her out of my mind, and concentrated instead on finding objects to line up to set my course. Half way back I recalled that I'd left the picnic on her table. If she came back soon, she could have it; if she didn't return until tomorrow it would probably have spoiled or have gone to the ants or rats. Pull. Glide. Pull. Glide. Heavy.

I left Bleak Point in my skiff at noon again the next day. It was slightly cloudy and not so warm. If nothing else, I was getting lots of exercise. I didn't bring any food this time. The more I'd thought about yesterday, the more I felt annoyed with her. Childish, because a moment later as I rowed, that electric sense of anticipation began to build. She would be there today. Her note had said so.

The wind was light so keeping the skiff aligned with my navigation marks was easy. Once again my sense of anticipation must have given my arms extra strength, and almost without knowing it, I rowed faster, with a sense of purpose. At the seawall, I tied up and went ashore.

She was sitting outside the house, and had presumably watched me row over. She wore an old shirt that had paint smears on it, and some loose-fitting tan pants that had been cut off just below the knees.

"Come look at this before the tide washes it away." It was another statement or command. Not a question. I wasn't sure where to look, but she got up and walked over toward the north side of the point and down across two rocks toward the water. I followed. When she halted, I looked down ahead of her feet and saw a good sized bass lying in the rocks.

She reached out her hand and held mine as she then knelt down on the rock, forcing me to do the same. I stared at the fish.

"I have this idea," she said, "that when you look into the eyes of the dead, you can see everything that it saw during life, and then when the mood is right, you can even experience it."

"That's a deep thought," I said. She turned and frowned at me, once again silently telling me that the comment was superfluous.

After that long pause, she sat down, but continued to hold my hand. "Sit for a moment. Look into its eye and let your mind go."

We did it together, but alone. The once-black pupil was now milky. But the eye still gave the illusion of staring directly back at me, and the fact that nothing on the fish was moving made the experience feel even more direct, as if that bass were frozen in place, with its entire attention focused on me.

I remembered Hester's words about seeing everything the fish had seen during its life — all its experiences from the moment of emergence from a slime of roe until its final death. I imagined the fish in its prime racing through that three-dimensional underwater space and looking for prey. But to be honest, I didn't feel I was seeing through the fish's eye; I was just imagining my own thoughts.

"Pull me up," she said.

We rose and walked back up to where I'd found her. I had so many questions, but couldn't ask. I remembered the other day.

As if reading my mind, she said. "Tell me about survival."

"I framed a picture; I finished an article; my brother is coming. I guess survival is going OK."

"And that's meaningful? Really?"

She'd asked me about *meaning* the other day; and now, again. I thought before answering. "No. The framing is simply a job to give me some free money; the same for the article."

"Stand still," she said, and she put out a hand onto my chest over my heart. She held it there in silence for what felt like a minute. "I find 'meaning' to be an elusive thing. Look," she said pointing, "there are no terns flying out there now. They were there yesterday. I try to find meaning in that — something more fundamental than that it's cloudier today. Do you see?"

By now I had relaxed. I could almost grasp what she was saying. I replied, "Do you think there's meaning in everything?"

"There has to be, doesn't there. What other possible answer could there be, if everything is connected? That's why I listen to breezes. They touch everything and then speak about it. Listen and you will see."

I replied. "I think about connectedness sometimes. Sometimes in the evening, I sit out and look at the stars. They're right there before my eyes, in a sense, right in front of my face. And yet they're billions of miles away and totally inaccessible. And in that moment of trying to balance those two thoughts, I have this sense that there is some connection — some real connection — between closeness and distance; between the stars and us."

"And yet you're not happy, are you."

"I wanted to be," I said.

"And now?" she asked, kindly.

"And now, I survive," I said. Once again she looked at me with those eyes that spoke everything while her mouth said nothing. 'I survive.' I had exited the discussion.

"Let's go look at something," she said; and she walked into

the house.

I follow her into the back room on the north side.

"Help me with this," she says.

I can do nothing but stare. The piece of canvas on which we had separately lain and then been outlined, was now a painting: Two bodies, intertwined, gripping each other. You couldn't see the man's face, but the woman was looking free and joyful, hair flying as they embraced, her feet off the ground, knees bent. And yet it was semi-abstract. The bodies were entwined in a way that was comfortable yet physically impossible, and the woman's hair almost seemed to radiate into the patterns that surrounded the figures.

"You did that? In just two days?" I stammered.

As usual, she ignored the irrelevant things I said, and replied. "Hold the far end. I need to tack this on the wall."

It was a big piece. After all, it had life-sized figures in it. I stepped back further to look at it. It was really, really good, but I wouldn't state the obvious.

"Come look," she said, taking my hand, and backing us up five or six more steps.

"I'm calling it 'Passing,' " she said.

I looked again. It was an embrace. "Why don't you call it 'Embrace'?"

"There are so many more interpretations of 'Passing.' It's more interesting. Try to see the two figures as passing each other."

"But they're not. His arms are wrapped around her."

"Not if they're passing in time. And that changes everything. In that case it's the embrace that didn't happen but that might have happened."

"But 'Passing' also means death," I said.

She looked at me. "What brought that to mind?"

"I don't know. Maybe the fish. Maybe other things." I stared at the painting. It was wonderful art, and complete; and yet beyond what I was looking at, was the memory of our lying, naked on the canvas — in truth, passing in time, but coming together in the painting as an embrace. And while the man's face — my face — was hidden, her face, the hag's, except she wasn't painted as a hag, was ecstatic. Joy pouring out and being offered.

"Let's get a lemonade," she said; and we went back into the front room. She opened a small cooler and took out two bottles of lemonade. We sat and looked at each other.

"When have you been happy?" Her words, though coming through an old mouth missing teeth, felt kind, and her eyes were soft as she spoke, so that the question which might have put me on edge in other place, didn't, with her.

"When I was a child," I said.

"What made you happy, then?"

I closed my eyes and thought back. An image of sledding with Arnold came to mind. I was probably seven at the time. We each had a plastic sled. Mine was red, his was blue. The hill probably wasn't that high but for seven and five year olds it was high enough. I have this clear memory of the two of us, bundled up, clutching our sleds and running across the flat place at the top of the hill. We threw our sleds down and fell onto them while still running. We flew down the hill, cold wind blasting my cheeks. It was exhilarating and scary at the same time.

I thought of the days swimming in the old quarry. The memory clip was that of leaping off the edge and sailing downward — a mix of thrill and terror, a sense of being free, and yet being dragged to earth. I was happy then.

"You were in the moment, weren't you," she said.

"I haven't even told you yet what I was remembering," I said.

"I find happiness is always in the moment."

I thought about it. I tried to remember being happy for some extended period of time, but I couldn't. Even if I thought back to something like Christmas morning, the memories of happiness all related to separate moments.

I thought I might turn the tables. "What makes you happy?" I asked.

"Your visits make me happy," she said.

"What else?" I asked.

"I'm going to answer you in this way," she said. "And I'm going to pay a price. Imagine that there once was a girl who had a favorite doll. She loved the doll intensely. And one day in a fit of pique over something which isn't relevant to the story, she sat in front of her mother and quietly ripped the eyes off of the doll. As it happened, the next day, the family cat — Freckles — was found dead in their back yard. The cause of Freckles death was never determined, but for months — and perhaps for the rest of her life — the girl's mother couldn't help associating the two events, wondering if someone who could ruthlessly pull out a dolls eyes might also kill a cat."

I stared at her blankly not grasping what the story had to do with what made her happy or why she felt she was going to pay a price.

"I don't get it," I said.

"Everything you know or suspect about a person or thing sticks with them and colors them whether it's true or not. You spoke earlier about connectedness. Once a girl's mother thinks her capable of hurting a cat that idea will always exist. In every future encounter there will be some little sense that she might harm something or someone. It's the same with everything else. Once I tell you about what makes me happy or not, or where I grew up or anything about my life, it will color and shape your reaction and response to everything else we say and do. It destroys 'the moment' by cluttering it with extraneous contexts. Does that make sense to you?"

This was the first time I'd heard her almost angry. But it did make sense! Part of the happiness I've felt being here on North Egg has been precisely because of the immediacy of the moment and the absence of context.

"I see," I said.

"I hope you do, because it cost me."

That was a surprise. "How?"

"I told you a hypothetical story about a little girl. But you won't be able to help yourself from seeking a connection, context, framework for it. A part of you will now surmise that the story was about me and you'll begin to paint pictures of a girl and behaviors that, fictional or not as they may be, have nothing to with today; with our moment."

I looked squarely at the ugly woman with the bent nose and missing teeth, unruly hair, and said, "I'm sorry."

"I'm the one who's sorry," she said. "I made the decision to ask questions about you; and you've answered them; and each question and answer was a wound to the moment. Let's talk no more about histories or facts today."

That whole weird exchange reminded me of something I'd read about or heard. I think it was called the Uncertainty Principle — something from physics — but the layman's interpretation seemed to be that in the real world it's impossible to examine anything without changing it. It had never made sense to me, since I knew I could look at a chair or not, and that decision wouldn't somehow move the chair or change its color. But I could see Hester's point in a way when it came to things you know or don't know.

Her face took on a fresh gleam. "Follow me."

She led me around the south side of her house. I paused as we passed by the two large boulders that from my house form the outline of a woman at night. But from here there was no such effect. They were just two large rocks.

"I want to show you my treasures," she said.

I couldn't imagine what she might be referring to, since we were headed toward the nearest side of the large pile of metal. But in a moment she stopped and stood next to a smaller pile of junk.

"I explore from time to time. You have to be careful, since it's not stable and many of the metal pieces are sharp. Others are heavy enough to crush a bone if the pile shifted the wrong way. I look for interesting things. For stories."

She bent down and picked something out of the pile. It took me a moment to figure out what it was. It was a broken, cast-iron sundial. I looked at it. She looked at me.

"It doesn't look like it tells time anymore," I said.

"Does it miss the shadow that used to sweep across it, I wonder," she said. "If it had thoughts, what would they be? Does it sense a difference between morning and afternoon as the sun first warms one side of the gnomon and later, the other?

She threw it back and picked up the head of an oddly shaped piece of what looked like stainless steel.

"I give up," I said.

"Look." She held it out and then dropped her hand, still holding it.

"Forget it. No sun. When the sun's out, you hold this one way, the shadow is an 'O', another way, it's a 'T' and yet another way it's an 'I'. I like that."

She was almost like a child going through her toy chest, getting joy from each object.

She took something else from the pile. It looked to me like an old Sony Walkman. No doubt broken; and in all events useless.

"What do you see?" she asked.

"A broken Walkman," I said.

"In one way, perhaps," she replied. "But pretend it's like that bass on the rocks and look into its eye, and see if it can tell you about its life."

I looked at it. Someone had written 'LF' on it in nail polish. Initials. And for some reason the name Lily French popped into my mind, and I pictured a teenage girl maybe thirty years ago or so. And then I thought it strange that something so old might be found near the top of a scrap heap this year. Perhaps part of the story is that the girl has moved on. Her aging parents, moving to the nursing home, have finally cleaned out her room.

I looked over at Hester who was smiling at me. "Open it up," she said.

I did so, and there inside was a cassette tape, something I hadn't seen in years. Phil Collins, *I Don't Care Anymore*. She stared at me while I looked at the cassette and thought about it.

"Why are you staring at me like that?" I ask.

" 'I'm a down disgrace?'.. 'I just can't win?..' You don't know it?"

"No," I said.

"Never mind then."

"Is there something about it I should know?"

"It's one way to deal with difficulty, isn't it. Just not to care."

"Did you take me back here to this pile to show me this cassette to suggest that not caring might be a solution? Something I should consider?"

She slowly shook her head. I could see that her eyes were tearing up. She might have mouthed, 'no,' I couldn't tell. It was as if some wave of despair passed through her. I knew I had said something totally off track, somehow missed the big point, disappointed her.

"Let's not look at the other stories in this pile now. Moments pass, don't they."

We walked back to the house. It was nice outside. I was afraid she'd dismiss me and send me off, but she said, "Get another chair and bring it out."

We sat facing ourselves and the sun at an angle.

"I must have said something back there," I started. "Is caring somehow relevant to you?"

"It's everything, isn't it," she said, looking off to some place.

"Well, I've always thought…" I began; but she cut me off.

"John. Do you have anything, really, to say right now?"

"No."

"Then let's be quiet and sit."

Then she added, "Sit over here, closer to me."

We sat quietly for an eternity, neither wanting to break a

fragile thing. When I finally was ready to leave I suddenly asked, "Do you ever treasure hunt after dark?"

She looked at me, slightly surprised, and then smiled knowingly. "Every moment is a treasure," was all she said.

I wasn't quite done. "And, I'd like to frame the picture for you. *Passing.*"

"Let's let the acrylic dry a couple of more days," she said.

CHAPTER Five

Days

We said goodbye in the strange way we were becoming accustomed to. That is, no commitment or agreement on what happens next or when or why.

I rowed back, using the sight markers and thinking about another strange day. Something about Phil Collins and a Walkman had almost spoiled everything. The moment had been something about caring. *I don't care anymore* had been the title of the cassette. Did I snap at her? I wasn't sure, but I'd said something like, "You think I shouldn't care, and that would be a solution?" As if I could simply wash away all the pain in my life by not caring? Was she suggesting that? No. Because when I'd spoken, her reaction had been to freeze up and stare off, in more sadness than I'd seen in her before. Could her point have been the exact opposite? That a better answer to life's challenges was to care more.

I tried to think it through. I did care, didn't I? My memory was burned through with a life of snubs and unearned refusals. I cared deeply about that. I thought some more. But there were different ways to care, weren't there; and there were different things you could care about.

I wasn't even back to Bleak Point yet and I was already missing her, wishing we could sit and talk about it. And I realized that in some strange way, I cared deeply for her. And she must care for me in some way. But this sort of caring bore no relation to my caring — sulking would be more accurate — about my own life. And then I scraped on rocks and was home. The reality was that other than these partial couple of strange days on North Egg, I didn't have much to care about.

I sat down at my old computer — thank god it's still running — and started to write an article. The ideas didn't flow, I kept feeling like I was falling back into my usual pattern of circles when what I wanted to do was preserve and extend the refreshing moments with Hester. I thought about the painting that I was actually a part of in such as strange way. I would frame it for her, and that idea alone excited me.

I closed up the computer and put on some nicer clothes. Half an hour later, I walked into Angie's Art. It was almost time for her to close up. She looked at me, no doubt wondering why I was there.

"Just checking something," I said; and I headed off to the back room where I did my framing. I'd ask Hester's opinion, of course, but I was thinking that *Passing* required a simple matte metal frame. I hadn't measured the picture but had a pretty good idea of how large it was, and was afraid I might not have materials that were large enough. I searched, and quickly found that I'd need to order something. I guessed the picture was about four by six feet in size. I'd use one and a half inch wide frame stock. I did have a sample — only about six inches long — that I'd show Hester before I placed an order.

I put it in my pocket and walked back through the store, whistling, although I didn't know it.

"You seem chipper today, John," said Angie. "What's the secret?"

Something just came to me and I blurted out, "The secret, Angie, is Life!"

"Life? Don't tell me you've found a life!"

That almost put me out of my mood. I had found a life, but it was fragile and personal and very short-lived so far.

"I... I... think...," I began.

"Tell you what," she said. "I'm leaving now. Let's drop in at Barley's next door and you can tell me all about it."

At any other time in my last few decades of life, I probably would have said 'no.' These sorts of invitations would end in my facing furtive glances from a surrounding public, wondering who let the weird cripple in. But I was in some sort of new mood. I didn't have to talk about anything personal.

In the thirty feet of walking around the corner I made the

decision to clear my mind and live in the moment. We walked into Barley's, where the air conditioning was too cold. It was early, so we ordered at the bar and grabbed a table near the wall.

"How was the day?" I asked Angie, and even before she answered, I regretted it. This was conversation as usual; this was history and baggage and old context. Angie would reply 'slow' and I'd then say 'too bad' and she'd feel obligated to talk about possible framing. So before she could even answer, I spoke again.

"I had an interesting day," I said. "I found a painting."

"A painting?" she replied. "What is it? Where did you find it?"

"For now that's a secret," I said, enjoying the mystery. "I think I'll be framing it though, and you can see it then."

"Is that why you're so chipper?" she said. "Is that how you found a life?"

"I'll tell you a bit about the painting, though," I said, trying to figure out how to keep in the moment. "It's about four by six feet. It's semi-abstract. When you look at it, it's an incredible embrace of a man and woman. Normally that would be a trite subject, right? But this is executed in a fresh way."

"I can't wait to see it," said Angie. "And you won't tell me where you found it?"

"I can tell you it wasn't at another art store or dealer. I met the artist."

"Cheers," she said, raising her wine glass. "We've each found an artist this week."

"There's one more thing about this painting though," I said, "that I want to share. It's the name: *Passing*."

"Passing!" said Angie. "I hope one of the figures isn't supposed to be dead!"

I laughed. "Nothing like that. But it's an interesting idea. And the idea is this. The two figures aren't actually embracing the way you see them even though in the picture it's clear that their arms look to be locked around each other. Passing means that they were in those positions, where they look to be together, but they were there in different times. Thus: Passing."

"What a strange idea," said Angie. "Can't wait to see it."

I desperately wanted to find something to say next — to continue the 'moment' or to create a new one.

"What's your favorite color?" I asked.

She looked at me strangely — but not like the strange-familiar looks from people watching my scar, but a strangeness drawn out of curiosity.

"Why do you ask?" she said. I could hear Hester saying 'Words. Defensive words.'

"It's blue isn't it," I said.

She startled slightly, and said, "Why yes! It's blue. How did you know?"

I could have just told her that it was because she almost

always wore blue colors — although how I even knew I remembered that is a mystery. Instead I said, "It just seems to be the right color for you."

We couldn't stay in momentness forever, and so she learned a little about my history, and I learned a little of hers – some of that context Hester avoided, and that doesn't really say much about the person. At one point I asked her what sort of things make her happy. Her reply was a total surprise, even though I couldn't imagine it leading anywhere. "I think one of my happiest times was square dancing." She looked past me into some place. "I liked dressing for it — like being someone else — and then the sense of flying freely around in a pattern. You probably wouldn't understand."

I pictured her. Younger. Full skirt. Maybe a checked shirt. Hair in a ponytail. And I saw her glee in my mind as she whirled around. "I can understand. It's that sense of being alive and being somewhere else, isn't it."

"Yes. That's it." And her face clouded over. I knew somehow that her thoughts had shifted to the reality of being stuck in that store every day, with slow traffic, clearly struggling for survival. I had already known she was widowed and supported herself. I didn't know her exact financial condition or anything about any friends she might have, but I was sure she had some.

"I think those moments of real happiness are special," I said, having just discovered it myself.

But she was now out of the moment and our glasses were empty.

"Thanks very much," I said. "This was a nice thing to do." I got up.

"Don't forget to show me that painting."

Friday it was hot. I already dripped sweat as I finished breakfast. I was about to get into the skiff and row over to North Egg as I hadn't been there in two days, but I had a thought, and went back inside. I opened the computer and called up Google Earth. In a moment I was viewing satellite images of the E: North Egg, Bleak Point, and Haddock Point. I shifted the focus to North Egg, and could now clearly see the main road, running up from where it passed J&M and ran past Osbourne's Scrap & Iron. I could even see the vast pile of scrap metal, and then, looking east to the ocean, I could see the rest of the point — the old house and some of the boulders. The property line at the north edge of Osbourne's property was a clear straight line, probably with a fence, but I couldn't see one at this resolution. There didn't appear to be any open road running into the old house, sitting at the neck on the point. There probably had been at one time, but after the house was abandoned, the road just became more flat ground on which to pile scrap.

And that left the puzzle. How did Hester come and go? She clearly couldn't stay there all the time. There was no power or water. She used it as a place to paint and to be alone (and to meet me). How long had she been coming? How did she find it?

And then I closed the computer, realizing what I was doing. None of those questions led anywhere I wanted to go. The answers — no matter what they were, would only serve to destroy the little aura of magic that surrounded my visits. In fact I could already feel the Uncertainty Principle at work. I had looked. And now my understanding of the point had changed; and I was no longer free to say to myself, 'Don't look. Don't ask.'

I remembered to pick up the piece of framing I'd gotten from the shop, and threw it into the skiff. As I pushed off, my depressed thoughts returned and dampened my mood, which irritated me, and depressed me further. I was half way across the little bay and I almost decided to turn around, but I didn't. My thoughts began to calm and slow down. I rowed more determinedly, which in the heat caused the sweat and drool to run free. I didn't care. Hester wouldn't care.

I tied up at the ring and hobbled up the rocks. No sign of her. I walked into the house. She wasn't in the main room. I pushed open the door to the art studio. She was in the loose shirt and cut-offs again, working on a paining on the wall — she didn't seem to use a traditional easel.

She turned and looked at me, smiling to say hello, and then noticing something in my appearance. She put down her tools and came over to me, studying my face.

"Don't say a word," she said. "Come outside."

She took my hand, led me back through the house and out onto the rocks.

"Close your eyes and face the sun," she said. "Feel the warmth and relax. Listen."

I stood there, eyes closed, hot, but pleasant, my eyes adjusting to the orange light on the inside of my eyelids. She stood behind me whispering into my ear. "John. I feel some tension in you."

"There is. There…"

"Shhh. Say nothing. Trust me. Take my hand and keep your eyes closed. Walk slowly. Eyes closed. I will guide you."

I had no idea what the agenda was, but my tension was overcome by curiosity and a little worry about what I might step on. I obeyed instructions and kept my eyes tightly shut. She seemed to be guiding me northward, and just as I was about to ask another question, I felt a violent shove on my back. My eyes flew open as I flew through the air and into the ocean. Even before I hit the water, I heard her cackling in laughter.

When I surfaced, I looked back, and called out, "You cheated!" But she didn't reply. She was stripping off her clothes and in a moment had jumped in with me.

"Don't worry," she said. I watched her swim out a bit and tread water, and then swim back.

"Let's get out," she said. I exited first — with a little difficulty since I was still wearing my clothes. I gave her a hand to help her out, and we stood dripping.

"Now, your clothes," she said.

"You could have told me before I got them all wet!" I said.

"But they'd be all sweaty. Now, they're just wet. A little salty, but just wet. When you're done, we'll lay them out to dry."

We were standing naked again, facing each other. She put her hands on my shoulders and looked deeply at me, finally nodding. "Yes, I think the strigil."

And for the next ten minutes she oiled and scraped my entire body. She declined my offer to reciprocate by saying,

"No time."

"Then I want to show you something," I said. I walked down to the skiff, bobbing patiently at the side of the seawall. Ungracefully I reached into the boat and pulled out the frame sample.

She nodded and then said, "And I have something for you."

I followed her back into the art studio where she pointed to a cylinder on the floor. "Yes, I want you to frame it," she said. It was wrapped in brown paper — enough protection from stray splashes so I could row it back.

It was Friday. I was back in plenty of time for Arnold's visit. I thought about taking a shower but didn't want to. My skin was still tingling from the strigil, and the soft odor of the oil reminded me of Hester. How could I have been so blind. Phil Collins. Caring. Hester was the most caring person I knew, and I had looked her in the face and suggested that not caring anymore might be an answer!

I changed into nicer clothes before Arnold came, leaving my dry but somewhat salty shirt and shorts in the closet to wear another day.

Arnold arrived a few minutes early. He was dressed in nice,

casual slacks and a turtleneck. He looked very dapper — unlike his older brother. Cancel that. Live in the moment for once. He looked very dapper. Period.

"Feel like going out for a drink? Or had you planned we'd stay here?" he said.

I had a modest selection of liquor and had bought some beer and wine, but with the weirdness of this week, why not break another pattern. I knew it would surprise him. He always asks me out, knowing I'll decline, and we have a relaxing time here in the cottage. Tonight we'll try going out.

"Let's go out," I said. "There's a bar up the street around the corner that's pretty good."

He was stunned, but being the polished lawyer that he was, he recovered in an instant. "Great!" he said. "I'll drive."

We walked out to his car. He cleared something off the passenger seat and threw it in the back so I could get in, and we drove the short way to Barley's.

Arnold took a look before we entered. He smiled and said, "Not the posh end of town, but at least we're away from that god-awful fish plant."

"And," I said, "The Chivas here is just the same as anywhere else, only a few bucks cheaper."

We walked in together. Unlike my visit with Angie, when the place had been practically empty, it was Friday night, and it was filling up. Numerous neurons in my brain were pulling cords to signal me to look down, avoid stares, to hunch over and hide, but I resisted tonight. The moment is the moment, and that would be it.

We sat at an available table and a fortyish waiter, dressed in black took our order. I had tried not to look and had tried not to be not-looking as we'd walked to the table; and I hadn't felt anything from the public. They were all absorbed in their own lives. Arnold looked a little preoccupied. Our drinks came.

"Jay, this is always fun. Cheers!"

"Cheers," I said, and added, "How are Marsha and Chris?"

"Just great!" said Arnold, and I immediately regretting asking that question. Hester would have given me a reproving look and pushed me in the water.

"What kind of meeting do you have tonight?" I asked, and then realizing that this question wasn't any different either — more context, normalcy.

He shrugged and smiled. "You know. Clients. It's always clients. And when you're their lawyer you come when they call." He winked at me.

A thought came to me. Time for a real discussion. "Arnold. You often lecture me about purpose in my life, with the implication that mine isn't going anywhere."

"Well, I don't mean, not…"

"Forget it. You talk about arcs — trajectories. Things with beginnings and ends."

"Absolutely."

"And they build up baggage along the way, right?" I said it quickly, and waited.

"What do you mean?"

"It seems to me that when you go down some path in life, you accumulate histories, memories and so on that increasingly shape and color what comes next. But I think they sometime impede it."

"I'm not sure I get that," said Arnold.

I tried to think. "Remember the story of the four minute mile? No one could run that fast until someone did, and then within no time at least three other people did it too. The theory is that until someone actually did it, runners knew in advance it couldn't be done, and that's what held them back."

"I see that," said Arnold.

"But it also works negatively, I think. Let's say you met someone you really liked. You had fun together, you seemed to share the same interests, you just simply enjoyed each other." I wiped a drool from my chin. "Now, suppose you suddenly find out that she used to be a crook, or a prostitute, or now had cancer. Suddenly you can't have fun in the same way anymore, right?"

Arnold put down his drink and looked at me with a serious smile. "Jay. I think you're becoming a philosopher. I've never heard you talk like that; and you seem passionate about it; and come to think about it, I haven't ever seen you passionate. What gives?"

"In a minute," I said, wanting to finish the flow of my thoughts. "Here's what I'm getting at. When you talk about arcs and goals and getting somewhere, don't you in a way destroy the moments you most want to preserve? Isn't it maybe like that Peter Principle concept, where you move ahead. You finally get to a job that takes full advantage of everything you have to give. For you, it's the best job in the world. And what happens? You're such a shining star, that you get promoted. But the new job asks more than you can or want to give, and you've lost what you really wanted. Isn't that the risk of arcs?"

Arnold looked at his watch, and then said, "Jay. You're different tonight. The brother I was talking to about arcs was someone who seemed to be lost in sadness about that raw deal that he got. That brother, has been soured for years, and seemed to just be wasting away. I've just hoped you could find a way to get your life moving in some direction. For me it was arcs. Work, et cetera."

I had to ask again, "But didn't you ever find unintended arc-killers — if I can put it that way? Or maybe it's something else, just some outside event that had no value, really, but you were curious about it, and once you dug into it, it upset what you cared about."

He thought for a moment, looking more serious than he had all evening. Finally he said, "Curiosity killed the cat." He then smiled and looked at his watch again. "I've got to run. I'll think about it and we can talk more next week. Did I say that earlier? I need to be back next Friday, so we can do this again. But as for you, something is different and you need to tell me all about it."

We shook hands and Arnold got up. I said, "I'm going to sit for a minute. I'll walk back."

On Saturday morning, I made my usual pot of strong coffee and fried an egg. On an impulse I took the breakfast plate outside and ate at the little green table. I had pulled the chair around before sitting down so that I was facing North Egg. I looked at the large boulders, trying to tease out a sense of the woman — and perhaps I was also looking for any signs of life, even though the house and its surrounds were so completely blocked that a lack of seeing anything meant nothing.

There was no doubt that I was different than I'd been weeks ago. That first encounter with Hester had jarred something loose, and seemed to have started some process. I was thinking now about things I hadn't thought on in years. I was seeing people differently and myself differently. Perhaps I was at the start of one of Arnold's arcs, or perhaps I was just finding unconnected moments that could be enjoyed, free of the contexts that had always dragged me down in the past.

I thought about the drink with Angie. It hadn't been planned. She had just asked me as she was leaving. Maybe I should have asked her. Did I actually have the confidence to do that? But in a way, even though I hadn't offered the actual invitation, she'd noticed a new mood in me, and that had been the trigger. We'd had a good time. Her favorite color was blue and she liked to square dance. Thinking about that made me feel good. But then I had the opposite thought. Suppose she'd said her favorite color was black, and that what made her happy was watching old movies where someone slips on a banana peel. That would immediately color our relationship. I'm a cripple. She likes to see people slip and fall. And yet, she wouldn't have even been thinking of it in the context of me, or she wouldn't have said it. Had she not told me, the fact of her joy from an old slapstick comedy would have no impact on anything we said or did going forward. But by making the knowledge overt, everything would be irrevocably different. I had to get that thought out of my mind! She hadn't said that. She'd said 'blue' and 'square dancing.'

The drinks at Barley's with Arnold were different from the past and in a positive way. I smiled as I thought of a new phrase. I was Hesterizing my meetings — trying to break out of the trite parts of conversations; moving conversations into the present. It caught Arnold by surprise, and I could picture his face again when he'd said, "I think you're becoming a philosopher. I've never heard you talk like that." Maybe I was. I certainly had a lot to think about. With Arnold, I'd been trying to figure out how to connect these stand-alone moments that I'd started to experience with Arnold's concept of arcs. They seemed in conflict and yet both had value. Arnold had been talking about arcs for quite a while, and I'd always known he was right — that I was following dead-ends and circles rather than arcs and that if I didn't follow an arc my life wouldn't change.

Suddenly I paused in my thoughts. Here I was, deep in introspection, thinking about drinks with Arnold, and I was only thinking about me! There was something about Arnold that I couldn't put my finger on. He's always in control, cool, and comfortable. But he wasn't quite as much that way last evening. Was it because of me? Maybe. But I'd rarely seen him look at his watch the way he did. And there was something else. When I'd talked about arcs being interrupted, there was something in his expression that suggested the idea was hitting home in some way. He covered it, but it was there.

Arcs and moments and the consequences of new context. My strange little adventures with Hester had changed my life. Maybe they were on some arc. I could already see a little bit of the rainbow. Hester...Moments...Angie...Arnold. It wasn't clear where it headed or whether it was multiple arcs, but I couldn't have had the drink experiences with Angie and Arnold if I hadn't had the experiences with Hester. Right there is a small arc.

But what about Hester, herself? She was a collection of moments. She resisted arcs — at least with me. She resisted histories, contexts, backgrounds, promises. She felt she was paying a price in our relationship by even telling an imaginary story about a girl. She always steered things back to the present, to the moment. Where does that lead if anywhere? It can only be thrilling to jump into the water with someone so many times. You can't keep doing it over and over. The thought made me sad. I loved my experiences with Hester. Would they just continue the same way until one of us got too bored? Or was there some infinite progression of moments that would somehow be sustainable but that didn't lead anywhere. Did I want the relationship with Hester, who despite everything was an old hag, to lead anywhere? If so, what might be the arc, presently hidden, of which we were both a part?

I shifted my thoughts again to the broader picture. I've built up such habits of being alone, of expecting rejection, of just living the cycle of the day with my occasional side projects, was there really any hope at this point of changing my life? I'd be trying to overcome years and years of habits that have walled me into the spaces where I exist. No. That wasn't the way to think about this. Thinking about it that way was to be the runners who couldn't break four minutes because they knew it was impossible. I had to move myself into some new moments, free of the baggage of all my thoughts about crippleness and droolness, and not reflect on embedded behaviors.

I realized I had one immediate next step, and it was a mini-arc of sorts. I walked back inside, put on some shoes, and picked up the rolled-up painting. I put it in the car and drove to Angie's Art. Angie herself takes Saturdays off, so I said "hi" to Frances and carried the painting into my little shop in the back room. Being Saturday I couldn't order stretcher and frame material today, but I wanted to measure it. I cleared off the wall where I had tacked up a calendar and hung the picture with four tacks in the corner. My shop's size prevented me from stepping back as far as I'd like to look at it, but even closer up, I found it stunning. Passing. Would the experiences with Hester — and frankly those with Angie and Arnold — simply be brief moments – passings – before life returned to normalcy? Or was I on an arc. Would the Passing turn into some sort of Embrace of life?

I measured the picture, giving some thought as to how to mount it, since it wasn't already on a canvas stretcher. I'd order the metal display frame and the wood strips I'd need to stretch the canvas on Monday. My notes complete, I left and headed out. I was whistling again. "Good bye, John," said Frances as I left.

CHAPTER Six

Mysteries

On Monday, it was cool and overcast. I walked past J&M and up the road to Angie's. I'd expected to arrive at ten; I arrived at five of. Another instance of the pace of my life changing. Angie was already in and smiled at me as I entered.

"Early today, I see."

"I need to place an order and then, unless you have some work, I'll be gone."

"Nothing new," she said.

I placed my orders and left. There'd been an opportunity to start up a conversation with Angie, but despite my overall changed behavior, it didn't feel appropriate, so I left.

I had no real plan for the day, and that brought Arnold and

his arcs to mind. He was right, of course. I would never really change my life without some sort of decision to head in some direction; and that brought Hester to mind and the curious directionlessness of our engagements.

When I got to the main road where I normally cross to then walk in the driveway next to J&M, my feet made a decision. They turned left, and I headed up the road in front of J&M and toward Osbourne's scrap yard. I felt a tingle of excitement and also foreboding. Did I really want to pry or learn things that she seemed to want hidden? I couldn't come to an answer, but my feet kept walking. They walked all the way to the scrap yard and then just past it.

There was a fence there along the property line. The piles of metal seemed to close off any access from the road to the house — just as things had appeared on Google Earth. But on the north side of the fence, I could see a faint path of matted grass that followed along the fence. That must be how she gets in and out, I thought.

At this point, my feet decided to stop making my decisions and with a sigh of relief, I walked back home.

I packed up some snacks and drinks and threw them into the boat. I wanted to see her. Arcs or not, she was a part of my life and a source of what I now was willing to call happiness. I was happy with her — strange as it was. I walked out and looked at the sky. Cloudy, but no sign of rain according to the weatherman. There was a light breeze blowing in from the east. That would make traveling to and from North Egg by sail an easy reach in both directions.

I walked back up to the rack on the side of the house and

pulled out the sail, boom and mast. It's a bit of work to assemble, but then again rowing to North Egg is a bit of work too. Finally, with the dinghy rigged, I pushed off, turned sharply, set the sail, and relaxed. This would be the first time I'd arrive sweatless.

With the sail doing the work, I studied the two boulders as they neared. I shifted my course slightly — to see if I could re-create the image of the woman in daylight. Almost. But it took a lot of imagination. I watched two seagulls in chase, one with a crab in its beak, the other hoping to fight for a piece of it. Where was the arc in that life?

Approaching the seawall, I lowered the sail and drifted in. I tied up with enough slack line to handle the next few hours of tidal change, grabbed the lunch, and hobbled up the rocks.

Hester was outside, painting something. The canvas was on the ground — and I supposed that that was because of the breeze, which might blow an easel over. She looked up at me and smiled.

"No sun, so I can paint outside," she said. "I saw your sail."

I thought for a moment that she must have x-ray vision since the bay is blocked by the large rocks. But I didn't pursue it. She must have walked out at some time to the end of the point.

"I brought some snacks," I said. "Are you hungry?"

She smiled again, and said, "Yes."

I sat on the rocks next to her and opened the bag. Now and then we took sips or bites of the drink and snack food. I watched her paint. I looked at her as if by doing so I'd tease out everything I wanted to know, but didn't want to ask. I thought of archaeologists who seem to see so much in simple rock piles or broken pottery. I thought of deconstructionists who claim to understand an entire book by reading the first chapter. Today she wore the same painting outfit she'd worn two other times. Did she ever wash it? When? Where? It didn't look dirty, just paint splattered.

I stood up and looked off across the ocean. Why was I doing this? I suppose because I couldn't help myself. But with this woman, something kept telling me — as she had told me — not to dig, that doing so would only damage the moments.

In a moment she said, "Please stay, but you can sit behind me. You distract me, there."

I moved behind her but at an angle so I could watch. Her palette was arranged mostly in yellows, oranges and browns. Once I was behind her, she became totally absorbed in her work. Every stroke seemed guided by a sureness that I know I wouldn't have felt. As for the picture, it was at an early stage and quite abstract; but I could get the general sense of it, and something about it exuded a tension between freedom and something else.

I watched her back. I could see the line of her spine through the shirt, the shoulder muscles moving slightly as she worked. I looked at her long, unkempt, gray hair. I caught whiffs of a pleasant scent — not perfume, just something pleasant. We sat that way for an hour.

The spell broke when she covered her palette with plastic and stood. I carried the painting and followed her in to her art studio where she put things away. She took the painting from me and set it on a rack on the wall amongst the other paintings. Some were the same as I'd seen earlier; some were new.

"Your new paintings are different," I said.

"Yes," she said. "Let's go sit in the other room at the table."

We sat down and she said, "Would you like to hear a story?"

Finally, I thought, she was about to reveal something of herself.

"Yes, please," I said.

And she spoke as follows:

Many years ago there was a foreign kingdom that was under the rule of a wizard named Spaylock, who had usurped the power of the king and kept his daughter, the beautiful princess, Alexa, prisoner. For years, suitors came from every surrounding land to seek the hand of the princess, and each was turned to stone on the spot.

Down in the village, near the foot of the castle a mystic named Durballa quietly raised his three sons, Abel, Bakkar, and Cafka. Over the years Durballa had carefully schooled himself in the mysteries of dark arts and spells and magic, while letting his small store go to ruin. With three sons to support, the family soon was in dire financial straits.

Durballa pleaded with his sons to help with the store so that he might continue his studies, and they all agreed. But as the days passed, Abel spent more and more time riding with his friends and Bakkar spent more and more time drinking in the tavern. It was only Cafka who was of consistent help, enabling the family to survive.

There was one thing the sons all wished for, and that was that they might find a way to free the princess and marry her, for rumor had it that if the princess could be freed, the power of the wizard, Spaylock, would be broken, and the one who married the princess would become king.

Durballa's intense studies not only hurt the business, but were damaging his health. He was getting weaker and weaker, but he pressed on, determined. And finally, on a dark Friday, he completed a deep understanding of Spaylock's power and its vulnerability. He called his sons to him, and told them the following.

> Spaylock will receive all who wish the hand of the princess. He will introduce them to her, and she will plead with them to succeed. He will then tell them of the challenge they must overcome. First, they will go down a road that leads to a place with six ways to go. There is a dwarf to whom you may ask one question. He always tells the truth unless you ask him a question about how to get to the golden tree, in which case he may choose to lie. If the wrong path is chosen, it will head to places from which there is no return. The right road leads to a rock next to a lake on which sits a beautiful maiden singing and playing a harp. Finally, the road leads to a golden tree which will speak and ask one question. If it is answered correctly, the spell is broken, the princess is freed and the adventurer marries her and becomes king; on the other hand, if the adventurer hasn't returned in four days, then he has failed.

The sons eagerly listened to this, but then Abel spoke.

"Father. It occurs to me that many who have come before us have died. What secret can you give us to save us from the same fate!"

The Father, who had grown very weak could only reply, "Two things, my sons. Know your goal. Trust yourself." And with that, Durbala spoke never another word and died.

The sons agreed to wait a day and then draw lots to see which one would go. But when morning came, Bakkar and Cafka found that Abel was not among them and had gone off to win the princess.

When Abel arrived at the wizard's palace, he announced his quest. Spaylock smiled warmly and said, "I see you are an ambitious man. Come meet the princess who will perhaps be your bride." He led Abel through the palace to a thick door, which he opened revealing a circular stone staircase. Abel followed him down three levels until they came to a cell wherein lay the princess on a feather bed. "Have you come to rescue me, the poor Alexa?" she asked. "I have," replied Abel. "I will return within four days, and claim the kingdom." "Then have these, as a gift," said the Princess Alexa, handing him fish and two small stones."

When Abel left the palace, he picked up his traveling bag and set off to win the kingdom. After one day, he came to a place with six roads, going in six different directions. He was now afraid, but saw a dwarf sitting on the ground. "Good man," he said to the dwarf. "Which is not the way to the golden tree?" Abel believed that in this way, since the question was about the tree, that the dwarf would lie, and point to the right road. But alas for Abel, his father had said only that the dwarf would sometimes lie.

When nothing was heard after four days, the two remaining brothers wept. There was much to be done at the store, and while Cafka worked, Bakkar secretly left in pursuit of the kingdom.

Bakkar went to the palace and was greeted by the wizard in much the same way as his brother had been. They descended the circular staircase together and he met the princess. She asked, "Have you come to rescue me, the poor Alexa?" "I have," replied Bakkar. "I will return within four days to claim the kingdom." Alexa then handed him a fish and two small stones in the same manner she had to his brother; and with that, Bakkar set off.

When Bakkar came to the place with six roads, he found the seated dwarf. He took the fish the princess had given him from his pack, and asked, "Will you tell me the purpose of this fish?" The dwarf replied, "That is one of the fish I catch here and send to the palace. When you look directly into the eye of a dead fish, it is said that you can see all that the fish has seen in its life." Bakkar took the fish and stared into its dead eye. He saw it swimming in a large lake and then swimming down a stream until it was caught. Bakkar looked around and saw that the stream came down the hill beside a treacherous path, which was the path he took.

He climbed for one day and finally came to the top where he heard soft music in the distance, and saw himself beside a large lake. And there he found the beautiful woman, sitting on a rock, playing her harp and singing. She was beautiful to look at, and her voice was like honey. She sang, "Aracka

Marixa drinks from the dew. Aracka Marixa's song is true. Aracka Marixa sings only to you. Bakkar was so captivated that he stood, listening for an hour, hearing the song over and over, but with each singing it seemed more captivating.

Finally he tore himself away and hurried ahead to find the golden speaking tree. Along the way he continued to hum the song he'd heard, which made his travel go quickly and happily.

He arrived at the golden speaking tree just before nightfall. The tree was surrounded by many stones, which he ignored. He walked up to the tree and said, "I, Bakkar, am here. Ask me a question." The tree creaked and groaned and finally said, "Bakkar, name the beautiful one you seek." Bakkar heard the question and thought of beauty, but knew that he sought the princess. However the thoughts of beauty brought the song back into his head and it confused him. Aracka? Araxa? Marissa? The names were tangled and he blurted out, "I seek Marixa!" and he was immediately turned to stone.

After four days, Bakkar had not returned and now Cafka wept. Then, he packed a small pack and headed for the palace. Spaylock took him down the circular stairs to the prison where he saw the princess. Their eyes locked and they fell immediately in love. The princess, governed by the spells on her only said, "Have you come to rescue me, the poor Alexa?" Cafka looked into her eyes and replied, Oh yes, Alexa. I will rescue you and marry you, dear Alexa." Then have these as a gift, she replied, handing him a fish and two stones.

As Cafka walked toward the place with the six ways to go, he remembered her eyes, as he had stared into them. When he came to the dwarf, he took the fish from its pack and looked at it. One eye stared up at him and it was as if he were looking back at the princess herself. The fish spoke to him. "I give you this message from the princess. Follow the path that goes up the mountain." The eye then turned cloudy and the fish was still.

Cafka gave the fish to the dwarf and headed up the treacherous path. To keep his spirits up he thought of Alexa. At the top as he approached a large lake, he heard music in the distance, but as his thoughts were only of Alexa, he knew he wanted nothing to distract him, so he took the two small stones from his pack and put them in his ears. He came to the rock with the beautiful woman sitting on it. She was singing and playing the harp, but he heard nothing and continued on to the golden tree.

"Did you like it?" she asked.

"But you didn't finish it yet," I whined. "Not fair."

"Well, it's obvious how it ends, right?"

"I guess," I said. "He greets the tree, the tree asks him the name of the one he seeks, he remembers her name, right?, and the curse is broken; he marries the princess and becomes king. Is that about it?"

She shrugged, as if disinterested and got up, coming back with two bottled waters.

"Why did you tell me that story?" I was bothered by the lack of ending, and only now recalling that what I'd expected had been some story about her life.

"You said you wanted to hear a story."

"But what was the point?"

She let out a small laugh — her laughs were a bit like cackles, but I was used to them now. "The point? Must everything have a point? OK, then. I'll say it this way. Everything I do either has a point or it doesn't. If it doesn't, then I just told a story that came to mind when you said you wanted to hear one. But if it has a point, perhaps the point is that in the story there are at least three things, three messages that you could find. But that would only be the case if there was a point to my telling the story."

She was almost talking in the same sort of Arabian Nights-like riddle language. "I'll bite," I said. "What are the three things I should take from the story?"

She smiled, "That would be telling, wouldn't it. Then there'd have been no point to the story in the first place."

She stood up. "I'm going to paint some more."

We walked outside. Despite the weather report, it now looked like it might rain. I didn't want to leave, but the wind was picking up a bit, and it would be stupid not to. She walked with me across the rocks and down to my boat.

I had an idea. "Sometime, when it's not about to rain, would you like to go for a little sail?"

"Of course," she said.

"When would you like to do it?" I asked.

"Whenever you like," she replied.

The first raindrops started to fall. I climbed aboard, raised the sail and untied the painter. Sailing away, I looked back. She was standing on the rock, watching. The wind shifted and I adjusted my course a bit. When I turned back, she was gone.

Thoughts were swirling in my head as I crossed the bay. She had given me a puzzle within a puzzle. The outer puzzle was the question of whether the story had any point at all. If it didn't then all of the talk about three things was just to tease me for her amusement; but if the story had a point, the inner puzzle was what were the three messages in it?

I knew about the fish eye idea, so that probably wasn't one of them. A wind shift suddenly tipped the skiff. I adjusted quickly and made a decision to think about sailing and not stories; but of course you can't tell a mind what to think. So as I more closely watched for telltale changes in the pattern of wind gusts on the water around me, my mind wandered. I thought of the painting she was doing. I wanted to know what had spawned the change in style that she'd used in *Passing*, and in the painting she was doing now. I wanted to tell her how great it was, but had learned the she resisted that sort of comment. I thought about the story — not the content or any hidden messages — but why she'd thought to tell it in the first place. My recollection was that it was just after I was admiring the painting, and expecting the next thing to be an invitation back into the art studio to look at other new things. But she had changed the subject and out of the blue asked if I wanted to hear a story.

I thought about how absorbed she was while she painted. I thought about her answer to the question of whether she'd like to go sailing. While painting, it was as if her mind were totally cleared of anything else; and as for sailing, she'd never mentioned a word about it, but seemed eager when I offered.

I was approaching Bleak Point. The rain was now coming down harder. The water took on that peened look as if it had been tapped everywhere with a small hammer. I dropped the sail, and coasted into the little slot between rocks.

Inside the cottage, everything seemed dark. I saw the little light on my cellphone flashing. It was a message from Arnold reminding me that he'd be back on Friday, and that he was bringing the drinks. I left the lights off and looked out the window. The afternoon was gone. My trip to North Egg had apparently taken almost five hours.

I stripped off my wet clothes, for a moment recalling the surprised swim last Friday, and put on clean shorts and a tee shirt. I poured myself a beer and looked north out the kitchen window. North Egg was invisible behind the sheets of rain. I thought about Hester and rain. Logic had convinced me that she couldn't actually live in that old house. What would she do in the rain? I'd discovered that there was no road — only a path along the outside of the fence by the scrap pile. Was she right now walking through the rain to another home? To a car?

I turned and walked into the dining room. I'd watch the storm out the south and east windows. My thoughts of Hester were taking me into other contexts that I was trying not to explore. I sat and watched the water fall from the sky, making patterns as it struck the ocean in different ways. I couldn't get the story out of my head. Cafka had succeeded where the other two had failed. Why? Was that what contained the messages? One thing that had been different between Cafka and his brothers was that he had actually been in love, instantly, with the princess. He wanted to come back and marry her; the brothers wanted to come back owning the kingdom. Know what you want. Was that one of the messages? Had to be. It was interesting if you thought of the message actually in that way. Know what you want. It applied to Arnold's view of the world, which was all about goals and arcs and attainment; but it applied equally to moments of happiness such as I'd found with Hester — moments totally disconnected from arcs, and yet the same message applied to each.

It's always possible to invent meaning from stories or experience, of course. There were numerous possibilities. Don't believe your brother, use every gift, even if it looks useless, like stones, avoid irrelevant beauty, always trust what a fish tells you, plan carefully for every trip, dwarves might lie to you, wizards are bad people. I could go on and on like that.

The rain made pleasant tapping sounds on the roof. I heated some left-overs in the microwave, brought them back to the dining room and watched the rain while I ate.

Tuesday morning it was still raining on and off. No way would I go anywhere in a boat this morning. I hadn't slept well, and remembered one dream which clearly resulted from a mix of events in my life. I had run down a circular staircase in search of a fish which, in the dream, it was imperative that I get before the woman prisoner would have to jump into the water. As I approached the prison door, water began to flow across the floor and slowly rise. The dwarf sitting there laughed. "You lied!" he cried, and disappeared. I looked through the bars and saw Hester. "Help me," she cried softly. "There is no one else." "As soon as I find the fish," I said. "Open the door," she said; and I replied, "As soon as I find the fish," for in the dream I was frantically splashing around, looking for it as the water continued to rise. Finally I felt a wiggle and grabbed the fish, pulling it up out of the water. It looked at me with one eye, revealing its entire life, and said, "Now is the time, but do not drool." I found the prison door and opened it. It was empty and the water swept me inside. The water receded but the door was locked. I rattled it, calling, "Help me!" And the harder I worked at the door, the more sweat poured off me, and rivulets of sweat ran down my scar and mixed with drool falling to the floor. I woke up at that point, feeling still trapped in a prison by my deformities.

I watched clouds move across the sky, not well defined, slowly changing shape. An image came to mind of those clouds sweeping across the window, sweeping across my life, and sweeping away the depressing memory of that dream. I thought of the long story the Hester had told me, and then of the new painting she was doing. I thought of my life: at one level it was still the same, and yet at other levels clouds were parting and new possibilities opening. Moments, and maybe some arcs.

It occurred to me that I was no longer having the dream about being panicked in an airport and trying to get things off my feet. But this new dream certainly wasn't an improvement.

I dressed and drove to Angie's store. The timing was bad. As soon as I parked the Toyota, the skies began to unleash another pounding of heavy rain. I pulled up my hood and ran, but entered the story dripping and certainly looking like some alien creature.

I looked up from under the hood and smiled. "Hi, Angie. Sorry for bringing the flood in with me."

She shrugged. "It'll dry. I'd mop it if I thought anyone would be coming in."

"Hey," I said. "You never know. Can't go to the beach. Why not go shopping for art. Right?"

It was weird. I'd no sooner thrown out that comment than the door opened behind me, and a young couple walked in, dripping more water as they came.

I headed for my back room, but as I passed Angie's table, I smiled at her. "See?"

I took my raincoat off and hung it behind the door. Six pieces of wood were tied together with string, which also wrapped around a receipt. This would be the wood I'd use for the canvas stretcher. I looked up at the picture tacked to the wall and loved it all over again. I began to hum as I worked. Measuring cutting, setting the angles square, fixing the mid-frame bracing. Due to the relative sizes of the picture and my work space, a lot of what I did was with things standing vertically. The last step was to attach, carefully stretch, and fasten the canvas to the stretcher frame.

When it was finished, I leaned it against the wall and admired it. The metal pieces for the exterior frame had not arrived yet, but the picture looked great.

I opened the door to the main room and looked out. Angie was alone again.

"Success?" I asked.

"I'll say," she said. "They bought both of the Coopers. I double wrapped them due to the weather."

Instead of saying 'That's good' or something like that, I said. "Would you like to see the painting?"

"The painting? Oh! You mean the one you were telling me about. Yes. Please."

She got up and followed me into the back.

She looked at it and remained silent. Then she turned to me. "This is yours? You said you found it and met the artist, but is this yours?"

"No," I said. "I am just framing it."

"I ask because this is real art. Not the sea-scene stuff we mostly sell. But I don't recognize the style."

"You probably wouldn't. This is an experimental piece."

Angie turned to me. "Let's get this out into the other room where we can position it properly with lighting, and then be able to see it from a little more distance. And then we'll have a cup of coffee together and talk about it."

Totally different from Hester, but a command, not a question.

Angie's store is three rooms: the front room, my framing shop, which is also our storage area, and a bathroom. The front room is divided by two six foot high partitions that provide additional wall space for display. Since the partitions run parallel to the front of the store, they create three areas as wide as the store within which to display things. Angie chose the side wall right up front. We cleared it, and hung *Passing* there.

It changed the whole look of the store from a commercial art store to a museum. True to her word, Angie brought two cups of coffee up from the machine in the back, and we sat.

I thought I'd better take the offensive. "Look," I said. "I'm an Art major. I know this could be a really significant piece. I don't know the artist well and have no idea whether it is for sale or not, and if so, what the price range would be. I'm not prepared to discuss the artist at all, but would love to sit here with you and admire the painting, and talk about it as a piece of art, if you wish."

"How long?" Angie asked.

"How long what," I said.

"How long can you leave the painting here. How long before you can tell me more about it and the artist. How long before I can find out if I might find a buyer for it."

"Maybe a week," I said. "Of course, if the artist wants it back sooner, that will govern things."

"It is museum quality, isn't it," I said.

"It is, and it may be more than that. You know as well as I do that it's refreshingly new – which is hard to be these days. Its value, of course, would depend a bit on whether it's a one-time fluke or whether the artist is producing more."

"I can confirm that there are more," I said.

"You are a man of deep mystery, John. A piece like this would surely already be known by someone, and if there are others, someone else must have seen them."

"I think it's all new," I said. "This painting was only finished in the past several days."

We shifted into a relaxed conversation about the painting itself and the concept of being in the same place but at different times. Angie had a lot to say about how the technical aspects seemed so strong and new. Eventually, we found other things to talk about. It was the longest time I'd ever spent in the public part of the store; and I don't think Angie even once noticed the scar.

Before I left, Angie said, "I'll put it in your work room each night."

"Why?"

She stared at me as if I were an idiot. "John. That painting is worth a fortune. It's right there in the window. I don't have enough insurance, and even if I did, it hasn't been appraised."

CHAPTER Seven

Merrant

Wednesday morning it's no longer raining, but it's oppressively humid. I want to tell Hester that the initial framing is done. And I just want to visit with her. I refuse to think about how strange the whole relationship is, and whether, if my brother knew about it, he'd call the loony-bin and have them come and get me.

I have a bit of a plan for the day and drive to the carry-out market and pick up a nice lunch for two. When I want to keep things chilled on the boat I use my trusty but beaten up Styrofoam box. A couple of years ago, Arnold and Marsha sent it to me for Christmas. That's how I think of it, but, of course what they were really sending was the frozen, mail-order cheesecake inside. I think I can get another year or two of use out of it before so many little white pieces break off, that it falls apart.

This will be a surprise for Hester. Of course, everything with her seems to be a surprise and spontaneous. I ask, "Would you like to go for a sail?" and she replies, "Of course," as if it were so obvious I should have already known. And then I ask, "When would you like to go?" and she says, "Whenever you like." Well I decided 'I like' today.

As I'm sailing to North Egg, I think about everything. Wanting to know and not wanting to know. The whole thing is impossible. I only met her a few days ago and yet she acts as if she's always there, happy for a visit, 'if I like.' She must have some other life — other than hanging out at that old house with no power or running water, and painting and waiting for me. I smile as I think about it — that little self-centered thought I just had. She's given no evidence that she waits for me. She seems incredibly caring, and yet, in a way, disinterested. For all I know she'd behave exactly the same if Joe Blow showed up and wanted to play checkers.

All of these thoughts evaporate as I pull into the seawall. She is standing there in a clean tee shirt and shorts — not in painting clothes. She smiles down at me as I tie up the boat.

I hobble up the rocks. She says nothing. Just smiles. So I say, "I thought we might take that sail today. To Merrant Island."

"I'm ready," she says, as if she'd known all along that that's what we'd do. Just like that first day. I remember what she said then. "I knew you were coming." No one has that kind of ESP.

We hold hands, helping each other back down the rocks. I finally have to ask, "Can you swim?"

"Yes."

"Fine, then I suggest you use your life vest as a cushion to sit on and lean back on." That won't make things really comfortable. Nothing is really comfortable in a small sailing skiff. But a moment later, we're off. The wind is out of the east so we'll tack to the island and then sail down-wind on the return. The day is humid, but the sun is burning it away; and, while tacking I love the feel of the wind in my face. Clear sky. Nice breeze. A strange old hag, whom I increasingly like, reclining near the bow, staring back at me, relaxed. 'What makes you happy?' This makes me happy.

"You look so happy," she says.

"I am. You escape to that old house. I escape to the water." For some reason her face clouds slightly, but I don't know why.

The way she's reclining, she's out of the sweep of the boom. I tack, and we adjust ourselves side to side to re balance the boat. On our next to last tack, we get a good view of the island. It would be more accurate to call it a rock pile. Wind storms and stormy seas batter it and keep anything from growing there; and cormorants and gulls sit on it and cover it with foul-smelling white gook, but it has one feature that makes it fun. It has a little cove where you can bring a boat into relative shelter. At the end of it is a short cave you can walk into — chest deep — at low tide. And someone at sometime pounded some metal spikes into the rock that can be used for tying up, so that you can leave the boat and climb the rock.

I don't plan to do any rock climbing. All of the bird dropping make it icky and slippery. So we'll sit here in the boat and eat the picnic lunch, and float gently in the waves. The birds who view this place as their property are flying in circles overhead, making a racket, but it will settle down in a few minutes — unlike the spring, when some of them nest here and practically attack you if you get too near.

She sat up and moved closer, so we could both reach the food and drink. We sat there, looking at each other. I saw a hag with messy hair, wrinkles, maybe a broken nose, missing teeth. I'd given up guessing her age. She looked old, but seemed to move like someone not so old. I wondered what she saw. A disfigured face that occasionally drools.

"May I touch you?" she asked.

It was a strange question from someone I'd been naked with and who had oiled and scraped my body.

"Sure," I said, tingling, and curious.

She leaned forward with an outstretched finger. She touched my face, gently, right at the bridge of my nose, and slowly traced her finger down the scar.

"I find it beautiful," she said, looking into my eyes.

I started to speak, but she removed her finger and raised it.

"I want to tell you another story," she said. And so she did, while we sat, rocking easily in the boat in the company of gulls.

There once was a princess who lived in a far away land. She lived in splendor and wealth. But her parents were evil and jealous of her pure soul, and they caused the world to close in around her. Their spies were everywhere, and every time the princess made the mistake of revealing some dream of hers, the evil parents found a way to cut it off and replace it with the opposite. When the princess wanted jewels, they gave her clothes; when the princess wanted to climb mountains, they took her swimming; when the princess wanted to learn about unicorns, they gave her books on real animals. When the princess wanted to learn to cook, they gave her lessons in sewing.

In desperation, the princess appealed to her uncle. "Uncle," she cried. "My life is in ruin. I am a prisoner and the world is closing in around me." She pleaded in desperation, hoping for some sort of rescue, but the uncle replied, "Dear niece. I fail to see your complaint. You are given everything a beautiful girl could want: fine clothes, the best swimming lessons, books on all the animals, wonderful sewing lessons." It was no use. She was trapped in a prison with closing walls.

One day a carnival came to town with clowns and jesters and puppet shows and all sorts of amusements. The princess saw her chance. Secretly, she arose in the middle of the night. She took lipstick and rouge and made her face into a clowns face. At the crack of dawn, she slipped out of the castle where she lived and walked into town where the carnival was camped. Soon she met the other clowns and jesters. She pleaded with them to let her join the troupe, but they were suspicious, and told her that unless she had some talent, she would be tossed out. Now it just so happened that the one talent the girl had was singing. She had never told her parents that she wanted music lessons. They had just been given. It was the one thing that hadn't been taken away from her. So she sang. Her voice was beautiful, and her songs were captivating.

She was invited to join the troupe. It was an exciting life, going from town to town, and singing, but after a while, she tired of it, and wrote to her evil parents. She said that she had seen enough and was ready to return. But they wrote to her, saying that there was no place anymore for a runaway singer, and despite the wealth and splendor available to the family, she was cast out.

In this kingdom where the story takes place, there are many bars with all sorts of merchants, travelers, bums and drunks. The princess left the carnival and began to go from bar to bar, singing for tips, or occasionally performing for a few coins. It was a tough life, and despite the beauty of her voice, her heart and soul became harder.

Her life might have continued toward more and more hardening of the soul except that one day, a witch chanced to be in the tavern where she was singing. The witch called to her and said, "I have a small home where you might stay." The princess eagerly agreed and followed the witch home. The witch brewed a curious tea and spoke these words. "I have looked through your breast and into your chilling heart. I have already seen the ice forming that deadens the will to live. I have seen inner eyes that look elsewhere than to the present."

The witch then took her hand, and said, "Let me show you

something." "What is it?" asked the princess. "Life," said the witch.

Hester stopped speaking. Once again, a story that ended abruptly. Neither of us spoke. But though it had been framed around castles, princesses, and witches, this was not an Arabian Nights story. I felt a chill as I realized that this must be some allegorical mirror reflection of some part of her life. For so many days I'd wanted some clues as to who she was or where she came from. She'd now given some clues, and it frightened me.

"Are you a singer?" I asked.

Her face remained expressionless. "Not a note," she replied.

We sailed back quickly with the wind behind us. Fewer words were spoken as I think we were each deep in our own thoughts and memories.

It wasn't until I was letting her off that I remembered the two things I wanted to tell her.

"I've mounted the painting, but am still waiting for the outer frame."

"Thank you."

"And I think I figured two of them out."

"Two of what?"

"Two of the three messages that might or might not have been in the story you told the other day, about Cafka."

"And they are?"

"One is to know what you want. And the second is to not be distracted by irrelevant context."

She smiled at me. "If there were messages in the story, those would be two."

"I couldn't decide if they were only one — that knowing what you want might be the same as not being distracted by what you don't."

"Don't over think it. It was just a story. But the two messages are actually different. All three brothers knew what they wanted. Bakkar let something distract him."

Wednesday evening I take my beer outside and watch the stars. I had really enjoyed the sail with Hester, but as usual, I came away with more questions and more things to think about. I absently rubbed my chin and flicked away a bit of drool. It had been an almost erotic experience when she'd reached out and run her finger down my scar. "I find it beautiful." It was the center of my vulnerability, my embarrassment, my difficulty in life. Until that moment, I had just assumed that appearances were off limits. She didn't talk about my crippled leg, and I didn't talk about her bent nose and missing teeth. For some reason, she had broken things wide open. "I find it beautiful." I heard those words over and over in my head. Involuntarily, I raised my own finger to the scar and ran down it. Beautiful?

And that strange event had connected to the story she told. Within an instant of calling my scar beautiful she had begun another story, diverting the conversation. I was learning that in a way she lived in or through stories. The treasure pile behind the house was all about stories; the adventure of Abel, Bakkar, and Cafka was a story having meanings I was still deciphering. The first story she had told was right after we had talked of 'happiness' for the first time. It was the story of a girl picking off eyes from a doll. But Hester had not wanted to tell it. She had said it would cost her; she'd pay a price; and she went on to explain to me her view that every piece of information or history colors our response to the present. In a way it was chilling, as if relationships were so fragile that an interpretation from a possibly fictional story might damage them.

She hadn't mentioned risks or prices today, but had clearly told a story that must have relation to her actual life. For some reason, she'd decided to lift back the blankets and give me a peek. Perhaps she'd been compelled to do it because she'd just touched my deepest mental scar by touching the physical one. What scar was she revealing? The story today had been about a girl, driven from home due to feeling trapped; who'd entered a free-for-all life. Her passport had been her voice in the story. As far as I knew, Hester's — if that were her real name — was painting. The life had deteriorated, but then she'd met someone — in the story, a witch — who apparently saved her. 'Let me show you something.' 'Life.' He knew that someone wasn't him. This was earlier history — if it were history.

Thursday morning I slept late, and spent most of the morning doing drudge work. Laundry. Taking trash to the dump. Sweeping rocks and shells out of the house and back to where they belong.

In the early afternoon, Angie called to tell me that the framing materials I'd ordered had been delivered; and that if my schedule would permit, might I come in.

Obviously she wanted something, so I got there by half past two. I was anxious to frame *Passing*, but wouldn't be able to go to work on it until I found out what Angie wanted. I was greeted cheerfully.

"John. Thanks for coming," she said, skipping all the peripheral chatter.

"Framing job?" I asked, looking up.

"Yes, but that's not it."

I could sense her enthusiasm about something, so I decided to be sarcastic. "You're firing me?"

"Very funny. Now. You weren't here yesterday — Wednesday. And you weren't here this morning. But guess what you missed."

I wanted to say something really funny, like, "A parade! Not a parade! Don't tell me I missed a parade!" But we didn't have that relationship (though in my mind, I now added a "yet.")

"Tell me," I said.

"The painting. It's bringing people in. I told you it was museum quality, and it's bringing people in. Most of them aren't even shopping for art, but they see it through the window, and realize it won't cost anything to step inside. I'm sure a statistician would say one day is meaningless, but we had traffic yesterday. And everyone who came in spent most of the time staring at *Passing*."

"That's great, Angie," I said. "I hope you got some sales out of it."

"Sold a couple of those racing sloops, but wait till I tell you..."

At this point she realized she was being pushy, so she said, "Take a minute. The new framing job is on your desk. The metal you ordered is next to the wall cabinet." Someone walked in the door.

Angie said, "Get that picture of yours framed, and then let's talk."

I was dismissed as she rose to attend to the customer, and I headed off for my shop, to build a frame for *Passing*. The other framing job was ignored, and by four, I was able to return to the display room with the magnificent, framed picture. We re-hung it on the front, side wall.

I went back to the shop and began to look at the other job she'd left on the desk. I could tell it would be a nightmare. Not that I couldn't do it, but that no matter what was done would be wrong. "Have the matting match the sky, only lighter." "Let's use a frame that has a gold glint to it, but a feel of something nautical." What the fuck was I supposed to do with that? I'm starting to like Angie, but sometimes she drives me nuts.

There was a knocking on the shop door. "John? We're closed for the day. Come on out. I have scotch and beer; that's all. Let's talk."

It was a command. I followed her to the coffee counter,

which, with a few magical pronouncements became a bar. I had beer; she had scotch, and we sat.

She looked at me, eyes glowing, and said, "I called my insurance agent today and raised the liability insurance to five million. I assume that's enough. I want to leave *Passing* on the wall at night from now on with a light on it. We'll be closed but people will see it if they walk or drive by. I know it will bring them in."

"Five million?" I asked.

"Look," she said. "I don't know. And I have other art objects here. I just felt I'd better do it to protect myself. It's a remarkable piece."

"I agree," I said.

"And you need to come clean," she said. "You joked earlier that I wanted you to come in so I could fire you. Don't joke like that; but since you're a part of this business, you need to give me more information on the artist. Other work he or she has done, what it's selling for, what the plans for this picture are, and on and on. You owe it to me."

I didn't feel I owed her anything, but I could understand her frustration. I decided to handle it in a way that Hester had shown me.

"Let me tell you a story," I began.

In an ancient kingdom, there once was a young lad who could draw exquisitely well. Everyone from miles around admired his skill. After many months, the king finally heard of this lad and summonsed him to the palace. "Young lad," said the king. "You must apply your skill to a portrait of my daughter." It turned out that the daughter had a crooked nose, and so matter how hard he tried, the young painter, who was so good at reproducing what was actually there, could not get rid of it.

In fear of being executed on a whim, the young lad sought the aid of a wise man. The wise man considered the situation, and said the following: "Young lad. You have exquisite talent for reproducing what you see as reality. I have seen none better. But you must learn to reproduce it as others see it." The young painter cried out, "Alas! How does one possibly see the world through the eyes of others?" And the wise man nodded and replied, "With onions. Squeeze onions over your eyes, and they will be brought to painful tears. You will see nothing like what you usually see, as your eyes will be filled with tears of pain. But as those tears swirl and blur in your eyes, you will see amongst the mist, a viewpoint new and fresh. It will enable you to imagine the king's daughter, not as you see her, not as the king sees her, but as she herself wishes to be seen."

"And that is your advice?" asked the young lad, worried about the prospect of such blindness and pain.

"Yes, my lad," said the wise man. "There is only one thing. You will gain a skill beyond that of any other craftsman. Your art will set a path for future generations. The king's daughter will wish to marry you, from joy. But you must never reveal your true name.

I stopped.

Angie looked at me with some mixture of amazement, curiosity, and perhaps, frustration. "That was entertaining, but tells me nothing."

I decided on a different sort of reply. "Yes, but wasn't that more pleasant than if I'd said, the artist says, 'fuck you.'?"

Angie wouldn't give up. "Maybe," she said. "But does the artist know about the little experiments I tried? When the first serious visitor walked in, asking about its price, I said, 'Oh, it's only here for display. It's worth two-hundred-thou.' And the visitor didn't blink an eye, and simply said, 'Sounds right.' So when the next one comes in, I said — lying of course — that it was on loan from Boston and was valued at two point three million. And I got the most shocking reply I've ever had. He said, 'If you'd told me anything shy of a million, I would have bought it on the spot.' And that's for an unknown artist! Now John. Do you see my dilemma?"

Oh I did. But for the moment, I wasn't thinking of Angie's dilemma, I was thinking of something else.

I stood up. "All I can say is, 'soon,' Angie. For now, I forgot I had something else I needed to do." I took out my cellphone and snapped a nice photo of the painting.

It wasn't very graceful, but my mind was brimming with an idea, and I had to get it written down or at least some notes. It simply wouldn't wait.

Driving back to my cottage I almost ran over a jaywalker I was so distracted. There was no doubt now. Hester was the front end of something new. Whether Angie's little stories were statistically relevant or not, it was clear that Hester's new style was captivating people. I had no way to talk with her today. We'd never exchanged cell numbers — I didn't even know if she had a phone. Tomorrow I'd have to break the news to her that she could be really big.

But it wasn't tomorrow yet, and that gave me some time to play with my related idea, my reason for racing from the store. There was a story here, and I was a writer about art. My mind had been freed from the prison of being the crippled freak. I was now in a position to announce something really new. This might even be the beginning of one of those arcs that Arnold spoke of.

CHAPTER Eight

Arnold

It was now Friday. Arnold was expected again at five and had said he'd bring the drinks. Thoughtful of him. But my mind wasn't on Arnold and his arcs, it was on Hester's art, and the arcs that it might inspire. The article I envisioned might even lead up to a complete book; or it could be a cover story in a leading art magazine, or it could be the introduction to a book on Hester's work. I didn't care about any of that at the moment. What I cared about was finding a way to convey the freshness and excitement of her style, while also putting it into the context of art history. And the hardest part of the second goal was that the art of recent years was a mishmash. Painting, photography, computer-aided art, computer generated art. The various directions which claimed to be important ranged from the wildly abstract to socially and politically messaged projects — LGBT and so on. The painters doing well commercially had fallen — in my view — into formulaic painting, as they reinforced their particular 'brand' to assure its recognition.

Hester would no doubt do the same. Abstracted realism across space and time or something like that. But it was different. It hit home in the today world. And it would see huge demand. I could feel it. Angie had seen it.

My article would take a lot of research — both to correctly describe the current trends and dead ends, and research with Hester herself as to technique, intent, meaning. I'd need to find appraisers and other experts to quote. I started outlining general themes and threads — rough at this point, but increasingly I could see a general shape as to how I might position Hester's art, and show what led up to it, and even where it might lead.

About mid-day I thought of Arnold's visit. I never felt a particular need to clean up for him, but on the other hand, the place was a bit of a mess, so I did a quick vacuuming and straightening up.

Arnold arrived promptly at five. He carried a bag of bottles in from his car along with a box of some sort of hors d'oeuvres. "Picked these up on the way," he said.

Arnold looked more energetic and alive than usual as if his life were at some high point. "You seem really up," I said.

He shrugged. "Things are good." He then looked at me. "You seem a bit up yourself. Anything new?"

"I'm onto something," I said. "I told you last week about a

painting. Angie thinks it's museum quality, and I agree. She even thinks it might be worth hundreds of thousand dollars."

"That's great, Jay. Great. Who painted it?"

I wanted to tiptoe carefully here. I still viewed my life with Hester as personal and private. "A woman I met. A reclusive artist."

We drank beer and munched on little shrimp and bacon things. I didn't want to talk about Hester or myself.

"How're Marsha and Chris?" I asked.

"Good. They're good, Jay."

That wasn't much of an answer. "Is Chris looking forward to school this coming year? I think I remember that he is one of those rare kids who actually likes school."

"All set to go," said Arnold. "New clothes — he's grown again. Still reads a lot. Gets it from Marsha."

"And how is she?"

There was something I couldn't read in Arnold's eyes. "She's good. Book groups, bridge, the club, redecorating again."

This was going nowhere, and now, half an hour into the visit, Arnold was occasionally glancing at his watch again as he'd done last week.

"I finally framed that picture. You need to see it sometime."

"Love to. I don't have time to do it tonight, but maybe next week, eh?"

"Sure."

We spent the rest of the time until six talking about memories — the quarry, hiking trips, the old car the family had owned.

After Arnold left I felt a little empty. It's always nice that he drops in, but there was some way in which he wasn't really here, and that made me feel that I was just a necessary ornament. 'Gotta see the brother when I'm in town — family and all.' But that didn't feel like the truth. Arnold and I were closer than that.

I cleaned up and got out a book. My cellphone rang.

"Hello?"

"John. Glad you picked up. This is Marsha. I hate to interrupt Arnold's evening with you, but I need to speak with him."

"Gee, Marsha. Arnold just left a little bit ago. He's not here."

There was a silence. "I've been trying his cell. He isn't picking up. Freckles died."

"Who's Freckles?" I asked.

"Our cat. Chris's cat." I jerked with a little shock since Freckles had been the name of the dead cat in one of Hester's stories. I was so stunned by this that I didn't reply.

Finally Marsha said, "Why did Arnold have to leave so early? He always tells me how much he enjoys his Friday dinners with you."

"I'm not exactly sure," I said, although I was already speculating. "Maybe you should try his cell again."

"I will, and I'm sorry to have bothered you."

"Marsha. It's never a bother. And I'm really sorry to hear about Freckles."

"A car hit him. And that was it."

And it felt like a car hitting me. The call ended, and I just sat there. Visits every Friday. A "client." "Gotta come when the clients want you." Short cocktail visits — not dinner. Every week, recently, which seemed unusually often for brothers who were close but not that close. Constant checking his watch. Arnold looking a bit more energetic and alive. He wasn't headed to a client. It was a woman. Arnold was playing around with some woman in town, and I was his cover for the visits. Son of a bitch. I pondered Arnold's parting words — said with a smile. "See you, Jay. Same time, next week."

Now I felt flat. Maybe I wasn't even the loved brother at all, but just the tolerated one because it was convenient. What did I think of my brother now? He had been the successful one, the perfect one with the perfect family. The arc of career; the arc of family. Was that family arc about to turn into a fizzle? Did Arnold cheat in other ways? Cheat at work?

I slammed my hand on the table for no reason. Dammit. What sort of relationship would we have now? And I thought of Hester's preoccupation with the danger of knowing things you don't want to know, and I couldn't make up my mind. Would I prefer that Marsha hadn't called and that I could just continue on, feeling a close relationship and a bit of joy that my brother chose to see me each week? Or would I rather know what I know now (even though I didn't actually know it for sure)? I shake my head ruefully. I think I feel more upset about what this says of Arnold's relation with me, than I do about the infidelity. Is the truth better than the myth? What is the truth, anyway?

Who the fuck knows. I drank too much that evening.

Saturday morning I woke up feeling lonely. I wanted to see Hester. I wanted to see her badly, I felt so alone, but I knew I also had other responsibilities. I got the pile of notes for my art article out of the closet and spread them out on the table again. I looked at them and just knew I couldn't focus on it right now.

I had the framing job for Angie which still needed to be done; and so, feeling almost lead-like, I headed for the art store. I decided to walk.

Angie greets me warmly. What a change — and I can't tell if it's me, or the fact that I'm the path to the painting. Either way, it's nice.

"Are you staying long?" she asks.

"Only long enough to do that framing job."

"Oh," she replied; and I realized that she was disappointed. "I thought you might stick around. You'll see first-hand what I'm talking about with how that painting brings people in here."

"Maybe I can stay a minute or two past opening," I said, calculating that it would take me that long to complete the frame. I felt I needed some excuse for her, for not staying.

"I'm writing an article," I said. "It's going to be a good one, but I have so many thoughts about it going on in my mind, I need to get back to it. Maybe by tomorrow I'll have the ideas sorted out."

"Have some coffee," she said. "I just made a pot."

The framing went more quickly than I expected, and I was done by ten when the store officially opened. I stayed around for fifteen minutes, chatting with Angie and thinking of Hester, but no one came in.

It's always a surprise to me, how my mind works. I really felt lonely this morning, and that made me miss Hester more than usual. My life is generally totally lonely, but after the awakenings of the past weeks, it was a shock to feel lonely again. I blame Arnold, mostly. That call from Marsha was a shocker. It blew away one of the few solid touch-points I had in the world — a comfortable relationship with a brother.

I thought these sorts of things walking back to my cottage, and through the smells from J&M. I looked in the refrigerator and took out some lettuce and vegetables and made a salad of sorts. It wasn't much of an offering, but I wanted to get going and not waste time at the take-out market. I threw it together, dropped it in the old steak shipping box, and launched the skiff. I had to row today as the wind seemed dead. Since I was in such a hurry to see Hester, I now, belatedly wondered why I had walked to Angie's Art rather than driving. I decided it was Arnold's fault again. Even with my crippled leg, walking is sometimes the best way to shake off agitation.

As I tied up, Hester was standing on the rocks in her caftan. What an incredibly pleasant sight — reminding me of that wonderful, mysterious first day. She stood motionless, but smiling, as I climbed up to her.

"Boy am I glad to see you!" I blurted out.

"Well," she said. "Here I am." Once again it wasn't the expected reply which would have been, 'Why?' And that stumped me as to whether I should continue or not. But I had to. In the past, if I'd had something special that I needed to tell someone, it probably would have been Arnold. As of last night, Hester was now the only one I felt comfortable enough with to just unload — even though our meetings had tended to exclude that.

"I brought some salad," I said, carrying the box over to the rock.

Impulsively, I grabbed her hand. "Look," I said. "I know we have some sort of unusual relationship. I have no firm idea as to its rules, although we seem to have worked our way into some. It's been a discovery for me. You've opened up my life again, and I don't even know how."

She seemed comfortable holding hands, "Thank you, John. That is very kind of you."

"But I don't know you!" I said.

She pulled away and looked off into space across the ocean. "I've told you I'm afraid of paying a price," she said. "I thought you understood."

"I'm trying to understand. I'm sorry. I shouldn't have asked. It's just that I'm depressed today. My brother. It's all gone haywire."

"Would you like to tell me? Don't do it if it will cost you."

I thought about. I couldn't see any harm.

"My brother, Arnold is younger than I. He's married and has a son, Chris. Arnold and I have never been really close, but we've been close enough that when I got fired from a job or had some crisis, I'd call him; and the same for him. When you've excluded yourself from life as much as I have, you have few places like that."

"John, it's stressing you to tell this. Can we go inside and sit while you continue?" She took my hand again and we went inside and sat.

"Recently, I've felt that we've become even closer — Arnold and me. He had started coming here to visit with me on Fridays as it coincided with visits to a client whom he said lived nearby. My meeting you has, I think, led to my being more aware, and more interested in life; so the Friday meetings with Arnold seemed to fit into that pattern as if they were another example of life opening up. I had this feeling that as I was becoming more alive, Arnold was more willing to visit — happy to see me as a happier person."

"And?" she said, as I paused.

"And it's all crap. It turns out Arnold visits with me because he has a mistress in town. I'm his cover with Marsha — that's his wife. He tells her he's doing the brotherly thing and having dinner with me, when in fact we have hurried cocktails and he runs off somewhere."

I finished. She said nothing. Was she thinking about it or dismissing it. I couldn't tell.

The silence went on. Finally she spoke. "That's it?"

"Yes."

She nodded. "You said you brought some salad?" Not a comment on the story. None. Her mind had moved off to salad. I was hurt.

"Nothing to say?" I asked.

"About what?" she replied.

I raised my voice. "About Arnold. About my brother. About his cheating on his wife. About... Aw hell."

She looked at me kindly as I sat there breathing rapidly and feeling like a jerk.

"John. Clearly, the telling of the story has not calmed your soul, has it. I wasn't sure why you wanted to tell it to me, since there's always a price. Were you hoping that I would join with you in some condemnation of your brother? Were you wanting me to be sad with you that your relationship with your brother has changed?"

She sat back and asked, "What did you tell me the other day?"

"About what?"

"About the first message you got from the story of the three sons."

"That you should always know your goal, and not be

diverted. Something like that."

"So John." She was looking at me with such kindness I almost hugged her, but the table was in the way.

"So John, What was your goal in telling me that story?"

I shut up for a minute to think. I hadn't given an iota of thought to why I was telling her. It was just the sort of thing you do when you are close to someone you're comfortable with. What had I wanted? I already knew the answer, but I was hunting for another one. I didn't find it.

"I wanted some sympathy," I said.

"I give it to you," she said as if referring to some physical object. "It's yours."

This was totally unsatisfactory. I had been dying to come over to North Egg to drown in sympathy with someone I loved. Loved? Was that the right word? I shrugged it off. And now I wasn't sure.

"You see?" she said. "You just paid a price. Your story of Arnold is devastatingly personal to you. It troubles you, and yes, I am sorry for that. But it is not my story or part of our story is it. If you want to sulk in depression about things in your life, please leave."

She stared at me. Hurt? Defiant? Questioning? I could not read this woman. She could change directions so fast, and yet she'd been so precisely careful about how delicate our relationship was. She'd created wonder from nothing and the most joyous moments of my life from the few strands of life I'd had left in me. I wouldn't lose this.

"Hester, I'm going to tell you a story." I have no experience creating allegories on the spot and had to think fast. "There once was a very lonely boy, and, I think, a very lonely girl. As each, in their own way, drifted deeper into loneliness, they each found a comfort by rationalizing their isolation. The boy, in particular, could feel the satisfaction of righteousness than his isolation wasn't his fault. One day, through pure chance — it might have been the sighting of something between two boulders that seemed to move, they met."

I continued carefully. "It was the young, lonely girl who recognized the situation for what it was, and devised a way for the both of them to confront their loneliness by flicking it aside, by making it irrelevant, by creating a new moment, a new existence in a space that hadn't existed for either of them. For the boy, it removed years of crust and fossilization from his soul; it created possibility."

I now softened my voice. "It also created a new kind of love— an affection deeper than he'd ever felt."

"That's the story," I said. "I don't know where it goes from here."

"She reached across the table and took my hand. "I liked that story. I think the little girl would like it too, if she heard it."

She then looked serious. "So fragile, isn't it. The boy and girl and desperate to preserve it."

"I framed your painting," I said. "It's all done."

"Thank you," she said. "Please keep it for a while. Come with me."

She stood up and I followed her back into her art studio. There were the pictures I'd seen before and another new one. But she'd been doing many sketches which were spread all over the place.

"When do you sleep?" I asked. "You've been very busy I see."

"It's coming together," she said.

I glanced at some of the sketches and nodded. "I think it is."

We went outside into the brighter light and looked at each other. I almost never noticed the missing teeth and wrinkles now on this lovely woman with whom I maintained this fragile life.

When I turned to go, she seemed reluctant to let go of my hand. "I wonder if you know how much the boy in your story must have done for the girl," she said; and let go.

I carefully hobbled down to the skiff with the Styrofoam box in my hand. We had never gotten around to eating any salad.

"I won't be here tomorrow," she said as her final words.

Once again I rowed home with thoughts in turmoil. Pull. Glide. Somehow the Arnold situation didn't seem as relevant anymore, and yet she'd never directly responded to what I'd said. In fact, she rarely did anything directly, which made her interesting, mysterious and more desirable for some reason. But all the indirection left many possible interpretations. Maybe there were no specific answers and the point was simply to find answers that worked for you. I couldn't undo the new thoughts about Arnold, but I had gone way beyond actual knowledge. Infidelity or not, maybe Arnold and I did still have ways to maintain a close relationship. Maybe he liked visiting even though it was also a convenient cover for his actions. Why did I have to always start by assuming the worst? That was what I'd done with my life. I got into an accident years ago, and ever since have blamed everything else on it; seeing ridicule where it might not even have existed; maybe I lost the jobs I lost, not because I was a cripple being eased out, but because I'd made myself into such a sourpuss that I failed to do the job.

And the more I thought about any of these things, the more I missed Hester. Weird. Inexplicable.

Sunday was a day off. Hester had said she wouldn't be there; and Angie's store was closed. Hester hadn't said where she'd be, but she had to have other things in life. I just didn't know what or where they were. While my first reaction was to take the comment as a sort of rejection, I later realized it was meant to save me from rowing or sailing all the way to North Egg, only to find it empty. Thanks, Hester.

I thought about the new painting in Hester's studio and all of the sketches — brimming with ideas, waiting to be realized on canvas. I wondered how rare it was that someone her age — I was guessing somewhere between sixty and eighty — would suddenly explode with a new energy and creativity.

Well, I wasn't anywhere near that age but I'd been living as if I were ninety. And now I had an explosion of my own. Just seeing those sketches re-energized the idea for the article. In fact it was at least three pieces now in my mind. There would be something in the magazine. A tightly written revelation of a new step in art from an undiscovered genius. There would be a book. There had to be. There was too much to tell. And there would be a biography.

"There's always a price," were the words that came to mind. The price of publicity would be unavoidable. Hester would resist it, but when you are the creator of something that has the power to change the world, it's hard to then stay hidden. It made me sad. Would I do that to her? Could I live with myself being the agent that would deliver her from obscurity to fame if she didn't want it? I tried to convince myself that it wouldn't be me. It would be the art — all on its own. It would be the paintings that reached out and spoke so strongly to people that access to the artist was demanded.

Lesson number one from Hester's strange story had been to keep focused on what you want. What is the goal. Right now the goal wasn't a book. That was a long way off. No need to fret about it now. The goal for today was the article, and I had all day to shape it and play with it.

By four on Sunday afternoon, I had a polished outline. It was dynamite, and to prove the point of all the words, the draft included the picture of *Passing* I'd taken on my phone. Even looking at the poor-quality photo gave me chills. I attached it to an email and sent it off to Graff Griffen at *Fine Art World*.

Done for now. I wanted to call Arnold and tell him about it. Maybe a week ago I would have.

CHAPTER Nine

Art

Monday morning I awoke refreshed. I realized I hadn't had any of the strange recurring dreams for the last few days. I was still excited about the article, and I badly wanted to share it with Hester. I checked the weather. Clear. Light breeze. I'd sail over late morning, but this time I'd bring a decent lunch.

I showered and ran off to the take-out market and got bread, cheese and two fruit salads. I went back and picked up a six-pack of lemonades.

I was off for North Egg before eleven, and on the way over did a lot of thinking about how I should approach the day. The things I wanted to discuss with Hester weren't stories or moments. They were thoughts about arcs in my life and I had a bad feeling about how they would go over with her.

About ten minutes before I shoved off I received a call from Graff Griffin at *Fine Art World*. He had received my Sunday email and concept for an article. He was thrilled by the idea and could immediately see what I had seen in the new direction. But it got better.

"John, I wonder if you could come to Boston on Thursday."

"Boston? Why? I mean I could, but what for?"

"I'd like to talk to you about a job here. I like your work. And I have a thought that if you were on staff here, you might help take *World* to a new level. I have no idea whether you have an interest or not, but I'd like to sit down with you and explore the idea — see if there's something that would work for both of us."

This sort of thing hadn't happened to me in twenty years, if ever. "What time?"

How do I tell Hester about this? Obviously if I end up with a job in Boston, I'll need to move. But that hasn't happened yet, and Graff hasn't met the scar and drool and hobble. And how do I talk with Hester about her art? Not about 'the moment' but about the arc of art itself and the role she might play in it? She's so private and hidden, I'm in fear that these ideas will be like a pin shoved into a beautiful balloon.

But I can't really do credit to the art without knowing more from the artist. How are you thinking about values, design, time, space, colors? And on and on. In the article I want to make her style and technique leap off the page. I want it real.

Pull. Glide. My biggest fear is that I'm now becoming selfish with a woman who has done nothing but be kind, and caring. I can't even begin to calculate the price I know I'll pay. Will it be worth it? Is there anything that is worth the price of destroying the very essence and magic that has so powerfully brought me from bitterness and despair and back into life? Is an article or a job in Boston worth that?

Crunch. I'm at the seawall. Literally. I tie up slowly, trying to shuffle my thoughts and clear my mind; and walk up onto the rocks, innocent and with no expectations. At this moment I want nothing to change.

I don't see her, and she's not in the front room of the house. But I do hear something.

I open the door to the art studio and gape. She has seven canvasses lined up along the wall. Each one has the initial outlines of shapes or figures. There is some progression in them that I can't quite pin down.

"Hi," I said. "I brought some..."

She didn't turn from her work. "Shhh."

So I shut up and watched. She was driven. I could smell and taste the ideas pouring from her mind. It was fascinating. I thought back to her comments about *Passing* — the embrace that was not an embrace except across time. In a sense the paintings she was doing here, in parallel, were perhaps also across time, but in a different way. I thought for a moment about commercial artists who get a formula and just crank out picture after picture. This wasn't the same though. Rather than repetitiveness I could see that she was exploring the dimensions and extent of the ideas.

She stopped at one point and just looked at what she'd done. I saw a slight grin form on her lips, and she nodded slightly. Wiping her hands on her shirt, she turned and smiled at me.

"Don't speak about them," she said. "They're still forming."

"Mum's the word," I said. "I brought some lunch."

We ate at the table in the front room. I didn't press her with questions about the new paintings. Instead, I watched the glow on her face. Seeping through all those wrinkles, it glowed. But finally I had to get to the questions that were in my mind. I thought I'd do it in a round-about way.

"I have a story," I said.

"I'd love to hear it," she replied, and put her elbows on the table, and chin in her hands, smiling at me.

"There once was an ugly rug weaver," I began, "who was burdened by bitterness. But one day he came upon a young woman — very young — whom he saw weaving the most beautiful tapestries he had ever seen. Now a tapestry is not exactly like a rug, but the weaver felt that if he could understand the magic of her technique that it might help him in some way. So he approached the young woman and spoke. 'I am in awe of the beauty that you create and have never seen anything like it. I beseech you to share some of your secret knowledge with me that I might weave more beautiful rugs.' The young woman looked at him with glowing eyes, for she was lonely and wished to share a part of her life. And she spoke. 'Kaba a cunetta. Ebba si jakka cordo ela hummit.' That's all I know of the story," I finished. "I hope it has a good ending, but I don't know it."

"But I do," said Hester. "It is a story that happened long ago and yet happens again in the present."

She stood up. "Come with me."

I followed her to the back room on the north side of the house. The door to that room had never been opened before in my presence. It was a jumbled mess. It was apparently where everything else in her private life here was stored. There were clothes, painting supplies, packaged food, bottled water, a cot and blanket, books.

"Help me with this," she said tipping down the end of a large roll of canvas.

We carried it into the art studio. She cleared the floor of various objects for the entire length of the room, positioned the roll of canvas, and then rolled it out across the floor into a long strip.

"What are we doing?" I asked.

'Kaba cumaja ebolaka paquer ela,' she replied. "It is where the story goes from here."

"But what does it mean?"

"John. You always look for answers in words. The two weavers can't speak to each other, and they communicate a different way. It means 'I can't tell you, but I can show you.' Now, raise your arms, and we become models again."

She pulled off my tee shirt and then began to strip off her clothes while I removed the rest of mine.

The first time we'd done this, it had been an out-of-reality happening. Now I felt the much stronger presence of the artist as she positioned me — hands, legs, even fingers, and then a turn of the head or twist of the body. Then she outlined it as before, and we changed places. Then we did the whole thing again. Sometimes the resultant images were similar to *Passing*, but others were quite different — for example the one which was simply seven different positions of my forearm and fingers.

She paused at one point and said, "Remember. The rug weaver wanted to learn. Watch." And she would then reposition things, or add lines or symbols that were some note to herself.

It was hard work and we sweated a lot. She brought out a towel and we dried and went back to work.

After an hour the long canvas was covered in images that would make five or six separate paintings. We stood up, sweating again.

"Let's get wet," she said, and took my hand, leading me toward the door and presumably toward the ocean as we'd done before. But as she turned, her foot slipped on the sweaty floor. I tried to catch and hold her up, but my feet slipped too, and in a second we were lying on the floor, sweaty body to sweaty body, faces inches apart.

She put her arms around me and laughed. "It wouldn't have been a good story if this hadn't happened, would it." We continued to lie like that for a minute, and then I rolled away. We lay on the floor next to each other.

"The tapestry weaver must clean up, and then display the secrets of her art." She got up, chuckling and walked out onto the rocks and dove into the ocean. I followed. Standing chest-deep, we wiped paint from each other's face and finally climbed out. I think she thought about the towel, but we both, silently apparently agreed to let the sun do its work.

Finally, back inside we both dressed and she went back to work. "Let's pull this back a foot or two." We moved the long canvas so that she could easily move between it and the wall with the seven paintings on it. I watched her work, sometimes puzzled by what she was doing, understanding it at others, making notes in my head.

She shifted attention to the canvas on the floor. She looked at me, and I think was going to offer some explanation, but decided to remain silent. She didn't start by painting at all, however. Instead she took a charcoal pencil and drew angled lines as if there were some structure she was trying to bring out, or maybe just to understand. Only when that was done did she grab brush and paint, and using the charcoal lines made some adjustments to the positions of arms and legs. There was some geometry in all this that was artistically critical to her, but that I couldn't grasp.

I had been thinking a lot about precious moments and whether they're sustainable. My moments with Hester were happening again, but with each meeting, some sort of subtle change would happen. Some of the things that thrilled and excited me and shook me out of my depressing life invariably became more familiar. Still pleasurable, but less exciting and less thrilling. In a way it was with Hester the way it had been at the pulp mill and with J&M. Something new is noticeable, but you get used to it and then it's different. It needs some other substance to sustain itself.

Maybe that makes Arnold right after all. Maybe moments in the end must fade simply because they are moments, and it is only through the substance of arcs that anything is sustainable. It was a troubling thought because it spoke of a need to move my friendship with Hester into something else, and I didn't like the thought.

We were both hiding a lot from each other. I still knew nothing of her other life or history; and now she knew nothing of my job offer in Boston, or my desire to show her off to the world and turn her into a star in the art universe.

Tuesday I returned to North Egg again. She wasn't out in front of the house, or in any of the rooms inside. I panicked. What had I done now? Had my insistence on seeing her paint driven her away? Was she ill? I went outside and walked around the house. I found her by her treasure pile. She was holding a small object.

"Do you want to hear a story?" she asked.

"Sure," I said.

"I am dust in the earth and I am a tree. I am a complex of colors, ideas, futures, and pasts. I am still except for the slow rotation of the planet and the sweep of wind through my boughs. A pounding by gigantic teeth rips me from miles of surrounding dust and transports me to a new place. I come at different times and in different ways but slowly collect closer and closer. Giant flames bring me to life and free me from surrounding dirt and grit until I am a beautiful silver stream, part of an endless cylinder. With breathtaking anticipation, I await the shearing slice and warm pressing grip, and I become five, and I know I'm beautiful, yet not complete. I lie with a thousand sisters waiting the joyous moment of completion. The humming of ripping chain gnaws quickly nearby. Stripped of periphery, I ride and ride until I am further freed from my future brothers. Spinning and spinning I say a final goodbye to what I no longer need, and joyously await a pungent, dipping swim into the clear pool. I see my sisters, and cry out with joy as we are finally united as a family, ready to go forth into the world and serve our purpose."

"I'm lost," I said. "I mean it was an interesting story, but I'm lost."

She held out the object in her hand. It was one of those little garden tools with a wooden handle and five prongs. She threw it back into the pile. "Everything has its history; it's story."

She started walking back between the boulders and the house. "But you're here to see tapestry."

"I'm here to see you," I said. "I'm always here to see you. Tapestry is the dessert."

We entered the studio. Incredibly the paintings had all advanced significantly. The series of seven that seemed to be a time sequence appeared done; and the ones on the long canvas on the floor had been cut apart, and the charcoal lines she'd drawn were no longer visible — all covered in paint. My mind was telling me now that there was a method in it. That the lines had somehow related to color values as much as space.

I watched for an hour while she worked, and then we sat outside.

"How many stories do you have?" I asked.

"Why a thousand and one, of course," she answered.

"Ah! Scheherezade and the thousand and one nights. A story a day to keep you alive."

Her face darkened and she stared off. "Something like that."

I figured the time had to be now. It would be dishonest to put it off any longer.

"There are things I need to speak with you about. I don't want to, since my time with you is timeless, precious joy. I have come to thrill at the way my moments here have a life that isn't damaged by other contexts. Or at least is only minimally affected. You taught me that, and I now find it is so precious to me." I paused.

"But..." she said, looking kindly at me.

"Yes, 'but.' The but is three things. One is about me, one is about me and you, and one is about you."

"Fascinating so far," she said — either with a smile or grimace.

"The thing about me is that I'm coming alive, thanks to you. But it has had consequences. I have an idea for an article that is so exciting that I sent it to my editor in Boston. He was so taken by it that he's invited me to Boston on Thursday to discuss an actual job there."

A happy smile crossed her face. "John, that's wonderful. I hope it turns out to be something you want."

Not a hint of disappointment that I might move away. But I couldn't pause now to think about that; I had the two other things to say.

"Well, I don't know yet, but wanted you to know about it. The second thing is the content of the article idea that I sent to Boston. It's about art. It's about your art. In particular it's about that incredible approach you took in *Passing* and that I see in the work you're now doing in the studio."

She didn't speak and silence filled the room until I went on.

"Hester. You're a great artist. I don't know how or where you got the talent and skill, but you've created something so new and exciting that, as someone who writes about art, I had no choice but to write about it."

"John, I'm glad you like it."

"No. That's not it. It isn't that I like it. It's that it's new, great art in a new form at a time when the art world is foundering around in retreads of old ideas. So it's not about whether I like it or not. It's about the fact that you've created something that's much bigger than me."

"It doesn't have to be," she said.

"I think it does. Hester. You must know how good it is."

I saw tears forming in her eyes. They weren't tears of joy. They were tears of someone paying some huge price that I couldn't comprehend. I had hurt her. But I swallowed and went on.

"And the third thing that I need to tell you is about *Passing*. You know it's framed."

"Yes, you told me."

"I haven't removed it from Angie's. It's hanging on the wall inside in the front. It is in every sense of the word, confirmation for what I just told you. It's bringing people into the store. Everyone asks about it, is thrilled by it."

"I thought you might just frame it there."

"Hester, Angie thinks it's worth hundreds of thousands of dollars."

"I don't want it on display."

"What!?" I couldn't believe it.

She paced around the rock for a minute.

"John, I am cold. I have one more story for you."

For some reason that sent a shiver through me. This would not be the Arabian Nights.

"A wizard and a dwarf lived together in a country where the only important thing was bubblegum. The dwarf knew how to make bubblegum, but did so secretly, so the wizard wouldn't learn the art. The wizard was cruel, but the dwarf couldn't escape since he was under a spell. Near to where the dwarf practiced his bubblegum art was a magic well. If anyone fell into it, all the bubblegum they owned would disappear. At the bottom of the well, was a hand-operated bubblegum machine that could make one piece per year. You needed twenty-two pieces to get out. Thus it would take twenty-two years. One day the dwarf saw the wizard dragging an elf down the street. At a corner, near an alley, the wizard conked the elf on the head and took all his bubblegum. In this country, stealing bubblegum was the worst crime one could commit. It distressed the dwarf to such an extent that he did a curious thing. He let the wizard follow him to his secret work place, but as they passed the well, the dwarf pushed the wizard into it.

The dwarf now felt free, but not forever. Soon he heard the voice of the wizard, spoken from the well, but carried to his ears by magical winds. "Dwarf, you have won one round; but no matter how much bubblegum you amass while I'm here, I will take it all from you when I am free."

I stared at her. There was some major revelation hidden there. She was dancing between two needs. One, to hide the contexts that would destroy our relationship; the other, the need to somehow warn me of something.

"Bubblegum," I said, but I wasn't smiling.

"Precious bubblegum," she replied.

I awoke Wednesday morning to the sound of rain hitting the roof. I had dreamed, but it was a mix of two stories. I don't remember all of it, but at some point there was a dwarf selling fish next to a well and telling me to look into the fish's eye and believe whatever it told me. He would hand me a fish, and it would be too slippery and fall into the well before I could look at it.

I woke up and lay comfortably in bed — comfortably because of the soothing sound of the rain, not the dream.

Hester had told me two stories that I was sure were disguised stories about her life. The first had had a girl driven from home who ran with the carnival. A witch had saved her from a life of singing in taverns where her heart was turning to ice. I still remembered the final words of that story. "Let me show you something." "What is it?" asked the princess. "Life," said the witch. In that story she had been rescued and introduced in some way to life — unless life was a metaphor for something else.

Yesterday's story was darker. The bubblegum made it sound silly — but it wasn't. Bubblegum, whatever it stood for in the story, was highly valuable, and the dwarf, who was being persecuted, saw the wizard stealing bubblegum from an elf. The wizard was pushed down a well for twenty-two years. It would take twenty-two years, but he would retaliate.

Something was or had been threatening Hester. There was no other interpretation — assuming that this story was really about her. She could never be the cruel wizard.

I have to admit I was in a bit of a huff when I left her Tuesday. The whole day was too serious. We were somehow at odds. But now, thinking of her as somehow the victim of a cruel wizard, I wanted to race back and hold her and tell her everything would be OK. It was raining and I wasn't going to North Egg. And I wouldn't be going on Thursday either, as I'd be in Boston talking about a job.

A gust of wind blew open my back door scaring me to death. Hadn't I closed it? Was this some new omen or story crowding into my world? A wraith, slipping invisibly into my life? I slammed the door shut. The obvious answer was that

I hadn't closed it all the way last night. There were some things in life that didn't have stories or meaning, and the wind blowing open a door, was certainly one.

I was up now and made some coffee and toast. I watched the waves and rain patterns out the window. I looked the other way, to the north, and saw the boulders that outline the woman. That was the image that had started it all. If I really forced it, I could see it; but it worked better at night when the Osbourne security lights were on, back-lighting the image.

I thought about playing with the art article. I had seen a lot of Hester's paintings and her technique since sending the email to Graff. But the ideas were still confused in my mind. I'd know more when Hester finished the paintings I'd seen her creating.

I called the heating company and made an appointment for them to check my furnace. It seemed a strange thing to do in August, but it was on my calendar. Now I could check it off.

Finally, I ran through the rain to the car and drove to Angie's. I wasn't wearing a raincoat, so I didn't drip as much when I ran/hobbled into the store. Instead, the rain had soaked into my shirt.

Angie looked up. "John. My God. Didn't you know someone invented umbrellas?"

I wiped my whole face — not just the scar and drool — on my sleeve. "Angie. Neither rain nor snow would keep me from my favorite place, despite my lack of umbrella." Where the hell did that come from? I never talk like that.

"No umbrella?"

"It's in the shop. Be fully repaired in a week. New snow tires and side curtains." Somehow my mouth was running amok on its own. She just gaped at me, laughing.

"Have them add windshield wipers and a heater," she said, still laughing.

"Any coffee?" I asked.

"Sure. Fresh pot, and I don't expect too many visitors today, between the weather and the fact that it's mid-week and the season is winding down."

I poured a cup and brought her one. I hadn't been in the store since Saturday. "So how are things?" I asked.

"Not bad. I keep trying to tell myself it isn't all due to that painting of yours. And it isn't. A family came in yesterday and wanted three seaside scenes for their den. But the picture is helping; and everyone comments on it."

"Any framing jobs?" I ask.

"Nope. I'm afraid not; but if you need some work, we could reframe some of those pictures I got at the estate auction. I hate the frames — old and heavy and dusty."

"I'm OK for now," I say.

I can tell she's processing something. She finally speaks. "Let me ask you something," she says.

I say, "OK." It's exactly the kind of question you'd never get from Hester. Waste of words, she'd say.

"I need a new sofa at home. I'm looking at one over at Schnaff's. You have a good eye. Would come look at it with me. I'll close the place for ninety minutes, and we can grab some lunch too."

"I'd love that," I replied. And I would. There was something about what Hester had done to me that seemed to enable me to cast off years of lead shielding and disappointment. I liked Angie. She wasn't exciting and terrifying the way Hester was; she was the comfortable and sweet type, and we had a common interest in art. Where was I going with this? It's only a sofa.

After we returned from lunch and sofa shopping I prepared to leave. "Oh, by the way," I said. "I need to call someone and have them move *Passing* to my cottage. I can't fit it in my car."

"Oh no, John. Don't do that. Don't do that to me. You still haven't seen what it does for this store."

"I'm sorry, but for personal reasons, the artist doesn't want it shown right now."

"And you're still so mysterious about all of this. Who is the artist? Is he local? Why not get the attention? I know this isn't New York, but we get pretty good traffic. Is that it? Are you taking it to New York?"

"Angie, I'm only expressing the wish of the artist that it not be shown."

"I'll rent it from you."

"It's not that. The artist just wants it not to be shown. That's all I know. It isn't about money."

"John. In your heart, you must know what a struggle I go

through with this place. In your heart, you must know what this painting does for me. Do me a favor. Leave it here through the weekend. Talk to the artist. Explain it. I'm sure he'll understand."

I crumbled. "OK. Through the weekend. I'll discuss it."

She warmed up immediately. "Thanks so much. And thanks for going shopping with me. And thanks for the cute story about the elves who lived in sofas."

I left. It hadn't been a good story, but I'd been exposed to so many lately that it just hit me; and she liked it. It was about elves, but a lonely one. I think Angie is lonely.

Later, I'm back home, missing Hester who is different from Angie, and wondering if ninety minutes with Angie was some sort of betrayal. No. Hester and I lived in the moment. No histories. No baggage. Right.? I poured a beer. It was still raining, but would clear up during the night.

The cellphone rang.

"Hello?" I said.

"Hello. Jay. It's Arnold. Glad I caught you. Been a hectic week. Lot's going on."

"Happy to hear it, Arnold."

"Look, Jay. I'm calling about Friday."

"Are you canceling? Something come up?"

"No, nothing like that. Still planning to come. But Marsha wants to come too. Says she hasn't seen you in a while and would love to do so."

"Hey, that's great. You want me to make reservations somewhere?" I'm carrying on this entire conversation as if the world is still spinning on its axis, while my mind is replaying the events of last Friday and my suppositions about Arnold.

"No. No need to do that. I'll do that...." Arnold's sentence just sort of fell off into a moment of quiet.

"OK," I said. "I'm looking forward to it."

Another long silence, and finally Arnold spoke. "Jay. There's one thing. It's a little difficult, and I might need your help."

"What's that, Arnold? Anything. Just say the word." But I already suspected what was coming.

"Last Friday. Marsha called you? After I left?"

"She did. She told me Freckles had been hit by a car."

Silence, and then. "But she thought I'd be with you, didn't she."

"She did. I told her you left; that I didn't know where you'd gone, and that she should try your cell."

Silence. "I need you to cover for me," he said in a flat voice.

"OK," I said. And then I unloaded — in a brotherly way, of course. "I'm guessing you weren't running off to a client meeting. I'm guessing it's a woman. I'm guessing you told Marsha you'd be with me for the evening."

I paused for a strategic moment, waiting for him to reply, and then interrupting him. "And now she suspects. She's coming with you. It's your way of showing that there's nothing going on. But if she happens to ask about last week, you want me to amend the truth a bit. Is that about it, Arnold?"

It sounded like Arnold was crying on the other end of the line, but I wasn't sure. "Jay. Jay. You're my brother. I need this."

We worked out a story. I didn't care at this point. Arnold needed me. I was a relevant brother again. Besides, I never did like Marsha anyway.

CHAPTER Ten

Clouds

On Thursday, I wash my hair twice in the shower. I study my scar and lip in the mirror. The scar has not weathered well with age and looks a little crusty and purple. If I were a woman I'd have some powder or stick that I could rub on it to hide it a bit, but I'm not, and I don't. I try to smile, frown, look serious in different ways to see how to best hide the disgusting look of my lip. I try different ways to suck in drool that won't be noticeable.

I dress nicely in slacks and a sweater. I have a nice, white handkerchief in my back pocket that I can occasionally use to dab my face. Maybe I'll claim a slight cold. Before I leave, I pack up the papers I've prepared in support of the article. I probably won't need them as Graff has everything electronically. In fact, at this point, I remember an old adage someone told me. "When you've made the sale, stop selling." Whatever I sent Graff already was enough for him to suggest a job. Don't bring anything else. He can't offer you two jobs, so the only thing additional stuff could cause would be to lose the offer he already has in mind. So I drop it all and decide to go up with just a resume, which I'm assuming is required.

Despite the rain, I'd gassed the old Toyota up on Wednesday. No rain this morning, which I appreciated as the windshield wipers on the car were getting to the iffy point. I thought about Hester briefly as I walked to the car, but she already knew I wasn't coming today.

There was no wind, which isn't relevant to driving, but which I noticed, since, with no wind, the J&M odors tended to creep my way, and I smelled them this morning. It was early. Not too many people at the plant. A guy standing by an old Fiat.

I drove out past the plant. I caught a glimpse of the guy who'd been standing there, coming to life and climbing into his car. That was strange, but none of my business.

I worked my way through town and out onto the main road, headed to Boston. A car raced past me. Gone. I looked in my rear-view mirror and could swear I saw the Fiat that had been parked at J&M. Was I being followed? If so, they had a long ride. And when I checked ten minutes later, there was no sight of the Fiat.

The offices of *Fine Arts World* are not ostentatious. Simple and functional, which is surprising to some, who come in expecting it to look more like a leading art museum. But it doesn't and isn't. Graff Griffen understands the difference between running a publishing business and running a creative art studio. When I walked in, I was greeted by Shalla Smithson, whom I'd never met in person. She was often the one who took my calls and has a soothing, refined voice with a slight Boston accent. It was a shock to see a slightly obese African American. You can never tell.

Graff came out of his office, smiling. He was a short man, wearing a bow tie. As he took me in, the smile never left his face — and didn't through the entire interview. "This is the place," he said, sweeping his arm around. "All of it."

He led me into his office where I expected to see the stereotypical pile of paper and drafts. There was almost no paper, but a large screen and computer. He pointed to a chair and we sat at right angles around a small coffee table. As far as I could tell he only glanced once at the scar.

I was curious how he would approach things. Indirectly, apparently. "John, I seem to recall that you did appraisals at one point."

"I did. Helping set ranges for auctions."

"You need a good eye for that," he said, nodding at his own comment.

"It can be a challenge sometimes, since so much of what turns into a trend — and thus value — is based on other things, such as the artist's story, or the passion of a single well-known collector. You know this Graff. When someone with the right reputation says, 'This is great!' then the flock follows."

"So, how did you deal with that?"

I almost laughed, remembering. "For me it was like a game, to be honest." I wasn't being totally honest. It was work. A job. Quantity and deadlines. But this was a job interview, and my life was opening up. "I got into the habit of handling the buy side and sell sides differently. For sellers it was all about encouraging them that the time was right; that the fad bubble might bust; that interest in so-and-so had plateaued. For buyers — especially institutions — it was about teasing out longer term considerations. Art that had staying power and substance. The auction house, of course, straddles the two, and the goal was to get the highest price. So scarcity became relevant. 'This is one of the last two that exist.' Things like that. It's funny. The arguments are different, but I always felt that everything I said was true."

Eventually we got around to the articles I'd been writing — not only for *World* but increasingly so. "I've watched your writing over the past two years," Graff said, now looking a bit more serious and business-like. "And what finally became obvious, and probably derives from all the appraisal work, is that you have a very good sense of what's actually going on. I get so much crap about which artist is fucking whom — and we do need a little of that — but I can use more good stuff about art itself."

The conversation continued. He liked my style. He felt I wasn't fully using my talent being an occasional writer and framer. He felt his business needed more of my kind of perspective. He needed someone more senior with whom he could plan and strategize the future of the business. He needed another pair of hands and eye to put issues together.

When I left, it was with conflicted thoughts. Graff had made me a nice offer. Assistant Editor of the magazine was part of it. But he also wanted me to work with him to extend the business into publishing.

"Magazine publishing is dying. Art magazines may last longer than some, but they're all succumbing to blogs and websites. I think we have a good runway, but I want to extend into a wider range of Arts publications — both print and digital."

I told him it made sense. He talked in general terms about compensation and bonus. It was generous and would move my life onto a new plane if I took it. But even sitting there in Boston, the very thought of moving my life from one plane to another called up thoughts of Hester. I didn't know how the plane we were on could be continued forever, but some new plane would pop the balloon and I didn't like the thought.

Here I was, thinking about the job offer I'd probably dreamed of, if I'd let myself even have such dreams, and looking at the man making the offer, yet thinking about how much I was missing my hours with an ageless old hag.

Graff started to frown as I sat there not replying. I finally snapped out of it. I slipped back into professional mode. I asked some follow-up questions to demonstrate that I understood generally what he had in mind; and I threw out some thoughts that occurred to me about publishing. I couldn't have done this a month ago.

After Graff nodded in agreement I said, "Graff. This is very, very interesting to me. If it's OK, give me a few days to think on it and come back to you with any final questions I may have. But I can give you an answer certainly within a week."

I could tell he'd been hoping for an immediate yes, but he was a pro and my request wasn't totally unexpected. His last question was, "Just tell me that you're not currently considering some other offer."

I tried to keep a straight face. Another offer? I hadn't expected this one. I've been burying my head in the sand for years; hiding from life. But I had to give him an answer. "I can assure you, there's no other negotiation going on. I just want to think through the offer fully. OK?"

"That's fine, John. Sooner the better. This will be exciting and fun." It might be.

On the drive back home, I missed Hester badly. I hadn't seen her since Tuesday, and I was living in this gnawing guilt that she had asked me to remove the painting, and Angie had talked me into leaving it on display. It wasn't that I wanted to tell her that — that conversation would be painful. It was that my guilt itself made me want to hug her. But it was more than that too. There was a selfish element. My conversation with Graff had rekindled my desire to really get into the essence of her exciting technique. If she wouldn't explain it, I wanted to watch more of it in progress. And then I felt guilty about my selfish feeling. I knew what I really wanted — what was more valuable than any new article, and that was I wanted time with her. I wanted more of what she brought to my life. I wanted more of her stories. She had said she had a thousand more. She was joking, of course. But I wanted to hear them all. I wanted to take her sailing again, and picnic.

There was a loud screeching of brakes as I apparently drifted into the wrong lane. I tried to rebalanced my thinking and keep some of my mind on the driving.

As I finally neared home, I recalled being followed that morning and it gave me a chill. It made me want to pause before driving all the way to the cottage, and perhaps that's why I turned at last minute and cut across at Angie's intersection and drove to the Osbourne site. I turned north and parked half a block up. The crane at the scrap pile was silent. I would see her. My heart rate increased. I wanted to hug her. For a cripple, it's dangerous to walk rapidly and I almost tripped. And then I stopped. The bike was gone. She wasn't there today — or if she had been, she'd left.

Dejected, I drove home.

Friday morning I was determined to make a wonderful day of it before Arnold and Marsha came. I wasn't looking forward to their visit at all. It was all for the purpose of covering up Arnold's visits to a mistress; and I'd agreed to help him do it.

I tried to clear those thoughts. I thought of Hester. From her stories I now knew she was hiding some important part of her life, and yet when we were together, that burden never seemed to intrude. I needed to learn that same skill. I wanted to push Arnold and Marsha totally out of my mind, and spend the day with Hester. I craved another magic day.

Perhaps due to my desire to get going and my intent focus on overcoming guilt, I didn't notice the car that had followed me yesterday until I pulled back into my driveway after picking up snacks and lunch. To hell with him, whoever he was. I hadn't been assaulted last night, and I'd like to see him try to follow my boat! The thought gave me a short chuckle.

I rowed over to North Egg with vigor. I tied up as usual. I had now mastered the challenge of the painter — leaving enough line so that the boat would still be afloat when I left.

I moved the Styrofoam box and another bag to the rocks and climbed out of the skiff. I looked up into the most beautiful sight of the week. Hester was standing there, looking down, smiling. I hobbled up to her. She took my hand.

"I am so glad to be back here," I said.

"It makes me happy that you're back," she said. "So happy."

There were two folding chairs set up on the rocks in front of the house. We sat. We looked out across the water and were seeing each other. Neither one spoke. We sat and felt the tingling warmth. Another precious moment for me, and I hoped, for her.

I popped the balloon. "You know I was in Boston yesterday," I said.

She didn't reply.

"*Fine Arts World* made me a nice offer."

She didn't reply. Shit, this wasn't going well.

"I think I'm going to turn it down."

She stood up. "Would you like to see something?"

"Always," I said, rising.

She led me into the art studio. Once again I was stunned. In the short time — a little over two days — since I'd been here, the art had progressed at lightning speed. This woman, who at times such as the past few minutes could be relaxed and easy must have painted like a machine on Wednesday and Thursday. To my eye, all of the paintings were now done.

I'll remember this moment forever. As an art critic, it was the most thrilling scene I'd ever witnessed. But it was paintings and art. It wasn't relationship. And just as that damned Heisenberg had said about position and momentum, I couldn't feel the emotional thrill of the personal moment with Hester at the same time as I felt the intellectual thrill of the best art I'd ever seen. For some reason that I'll leave to the psychologists to explain, they were incompatible.

If I remained the art critic and famous author of the great, new article and book; or the great new Assistant Editor of *Fine Arts World*, I would plunge into interrogating her about technique; I'd burden her with questions about where she learned her skills. And that would lead into the broader questions. Who are you? Why paint here rather than in a real studio? What's going on!

But if I wasn't that person. If I were simply Hester's neighbor, who found her company to be the most exciting thing in my life, I couldn't do that. We would be finding some new way to experience the moment; perhaps some new story; perhaps a look at more treasures.

They were not compatible. So for that day I made a decision. To hell with the article and my demands to watch her technique or to hear about it. There was something — fragile as it was — that was more important to me.

I think Hester may even have been expecting me to dig in with comments and questions about the paintings. Where she might have been displaying a look of exhilaration and pride, her look was more one of resignation. Expecting the drudgery of a technical discussion of art.

I held her shoulders and turned her toward me. "Hester. Have I told you how much I love you?"

As stoic as she sometimes had been, it was totally unexpected and she melted.

She had no breasts left, but I could see them rising and falling as she looked at me, silent, smiling.

"I told you a story the other day about a witch and a princess. Do you remember?"

"I do." Spoken almost as a marriage vow.

"The witch had said 'Let me show you something.' The princess asked, 'What is it?' and the witch replied, 'Life.'

Her eyes were now wet as she stared into mine. "You are the most important thing in my life, John."

She fell against me and I hugged her. Whatever must have been bottled up inside for all these days came pouring out. Not in words but in tears and sobs. She lay against my chest, my face buried in her messy hair, drool probably slobbering into it, and she cried.

We stood there for an endless time. I thought of what a wonderful person this was, while she poured out the story of her life in words I couldn't understand — the foreign language whose words are tears.

I didn't know what to think and didn't want to think. I wanted time to stop. But it doesn't.

She stopped crying and looked up at me, eyes wet and cheeks wet. For some reason she ran a finger down my scar, but said nothing. At a moment like this, what could be said?

There was a racket and we both looked up to see two gulls fighting in the air over a crab.

"Can I tell you something?" I said.

"Of course."

"I used to sit on the rocks out by the water, by my cottage, and watch the terns and gulls. I used to watch the gulls fight for morsels of food. That used to be my metric."

"Metric for what?" she asked.

"Metric for life. I used to try to overcome despair about my own life by realizing that it wasn't as bad as being a gull."

She didn't say anything.

"Pathetic, huh?"

"If you want it to be," she said.

That one threw me. "I didn't want my life to be that bad. It just was."

She didn't say anything, and I finally thought I understood. My life was only good or bad by comparison because I chose to look at things that way. No one forced me to choose seagulls as a metric for happiness in life. I had chosen them as a way to punish myself and keep myself pinned in unhappiness.

"The choices we make," I said.

"Oh, yes. The choices we make," she replied.

And we both looked back into our lives, willing the past to stay put for another day, another hour, another minute.

It looked like she spotted something of interest near the water and walked over to get it. It was a scallop shell which she held out to me.

"Do you ever wonder if shells were actually used for money?"

"I haven't thought about it," I said.

"Think of how rich we'd be."

"I heard a joke once," I said.

"Tell me."

"There was a boy who had a mangy dog as a pet. The boy was poor but enterprising. He decided he wanted a million dollars, so he walked into a bank and up to the bank president and said 'I want a million dollars.' And the bank president replied, 'Why would I give you a million dollars?' The boy replied, 'because I'll sell you my million dollar dog. It's a fair deal.' The bank president laughed and said, 'Get out. You'll never get a million for that mutt. You won't get fifty.' The boy left, dejected. But a few days later, the bank president saw him walking up the street, happy as a clam. 'Why so happy?' he asked. 'Cause I finally sold my dog,' said the boy. 'How much did you get?' asked the bank president smiling, and expecting the boy to name a low number. 'I got a million for it,' said the boy. 'That's why I'm so happy!' 'A million!' said the bank president incredulously. 'You got a million dollars for that mangy mutt?' 'Yep,' said the boy. 'I traded him for two five hundred thousand dollar cats!' "

Hester laughed. "What do you suppose we could trade this million dollar shell for?" she asked.

I followed her back to her treasure pile where she laid the shell.

She rummaged around for a second and pulled out a metal box. It was about six by eight inches and a couple of inches high. It was dirty and had a dent in one corner, but at some time had been an object of beauty as intricate designs had been etched into it. There was a small padlock that held the clasp closed.

"What do you think?" she said, holding it out to me.

"It would look quite nice if it were cleaned up."

"It would. Take it."

I took the box and turned it to look at the different sides. As I did so, I could feel and hear things shifting around inside. "What's in it, I wonder?" I said.

"You see? It's a metaphor for life isn't it? Isn't it wonderful?"

I thought about it, and let out a quick smile when I realized my first words had been 'It would be quite nice if it were cleaned up.' That certainly applied to a lot of lives. But like Hester's and my lives, there were the hidden parts too.

"Do you want to open it?" I asked.

"Do you?" she countered.

"I don't know," I said. "That's the thing, isn't it? When you don't know what you don't know you don't know if you want to know."

"I like to think about opening it, but not doing so. That allows all the possibilities to remain, all the stories of what might be to be told."

"It's more valuable that way, isn't it," I said.

"Even that is something I don't know. It might contain something I've craved all my life, in which case, that might be worth more than the uncertainty and stories."

"It's like us, isn't it. We talk in stories, but we actually know little."

"I like to think we know everything," she said. "Everything that wants to be known. For me that sort of everything is the one that opens infinite possibility."

I didn't quite get it, but it was a beautiful thought, and it gave me a physical thrill of happiness just to be imagining infinite possibilities with her. I handed the box back.

"I didn't make myself clear, did I?" she asked.

"Not entirely," I said.

She almost grinned at me. "Then I must try to explain it with a story. But let's go back inside and sit."

We walked in and sat. I opened up the food I'd brought, and we each had a bite before she began.

"There once was an evil kingdom, ruled by an evil prince. Each year, he would round up three peasants and condemn them all to death. But he did it in the strangest way. In January, he would selected the first one, and attach a spell to him, saying, 'On the last day of the year, you will die. There is no escape.' Months would go by and then in September he would select a second peasant, cast the spell and say the same thing — but now, of course, there were only three months left in the year. Finally, half way through December, he would select the third peasant and do the same thing." She paused.

"You're not done yet are you?" I asked.

"For me, the story stops there, but the conversation doesn't. Pick a month, say, July. Which of the three might be happier? Certainly the third peasant since he has no inkling of his fate. He's happy living in uncertainty even though he might fall from a tractor the next day and die. The first peasant has been fretting about his fate all year, but has had time to make plans."

She smiled at me. "I don't want to spend any more time on that story except to think about the final peasant. Suppose he has such control of his mind that he can push thoughts of fate away and focus on living. Isn't he then, the happiest?"

"Why are you telling me this?" I asked.

She shrugged. "No matter. I think things like that when I look at that box. It helps me."

She stood up. "I know you also came to see the paintings. That's part of your box that is open now; some knowledge I have of you that shades everything else. When you come here, I now can always wonder if it was me or the art."

I grabbed her arm, but softly. "Hester, let me tell you a quick story. Once there was a woman who was loved by a man. He thrilled every time he was with her. It was such a thrill that even though there were all sorts of other distractions in his life, he always focused is love and hopes on the woman. One day, however, he discovered that she had a million dollar shell. In fact that she could make as many million dollar shells as she wanted. His love for the woman never wavered, but from that moment on, the value of the shells and the potential they offered could no longer be ignored."

I paused, but she didn't interrupt. I finished this way. "Although the man's love never wavered, the woman began to feel that something important had changed, and as she started to feel that way, it caused him to feel the change. Finally, the man said to the woman, 'If I thought my fondness for shells might cause me to lose you and the magic we share, I would smash every one of them.' That's what he said. Of course, it's only a story."

She leaned forward and kissed me. "Would you like to see the pictures again?"

I would love to see the pictures again — pictures that electrified the air around them.

"Not now," I said. "I saw them this morning." *They are the greatest things in art at the moment.*

"I think I'd rather spend the rest of the afternoon with you. We'll leave the art inside the box, OK?"

She smiled and gave me another quick kiss. "You know you can't really put things back in the box, but thank you."

We walk back outside and sit in the folding chairs. We seemingly talk for hours. I can't remember a time when I felt freer or more relaxed or more at home.

"I'm giving it to you," she said, looking off.

"Giving me what?"

"*Passing.* The painting. It's yours."

Two lightning bolts fly through my mind and collide. One is the shock that she would even think of giving that painting up to me; and the second is the greater guilt I now feel for not taking it off display as promised.

"I'm stunned," I said. "You can't do that. It's too valuable."

Her face clouded. "Please just say, 'Thank you.' That's all."

And with that she'd cut off the entire conversation that would have happened where we both try to argue around a gift. But there was no stronger way she could have said that not only was she giving it to me, but that to her, it was important that she do so.

"Thank you, from the bottom of my heart," I said.

I had to stand up at that point and walk around. The thought of that gift was too energizing. And my thoughts didn't fly to the art and what I'd do with it, but stayed locked onto Hester and what an incredible, caring person she was; and how essential to my life.

I wanted time to stand still, but it doesn't. I finally glanced at my watch. Three-thirty. I needed to head back, shower and get ready for Arnold and Marsha. The thought of that was so polluting to the mood that I almost decided to let my brother fend for himself and just stay here but I couldn't.

We were standing up as I readied to leave. I was putting the lid back on the Styrofoam box, and she was staring off to the north.

Suddenly I heard a gasp, and she grabbed my hand.

"What?" I said.

"I…I just thought of something."

It felt like she'd started to say something else and then changed her mind.

"You're always thinking of something else — a thousand and one stories right?"

"Right," she said. But she wasn't smiling. I held her hand and it shivered slightly.

"Take me with you," she said.

I stared at her. "Now? In the boat?"

"Yes," she said.

There was nothing at that moment that I would rather do than take her with me. It had always been a thought. But Arnold and Marsha were coming and the point of the evening was to plaster over Arnold's infidelity. How would it play if I showed up with an unknown old woman?

"I can't do it today. I'll come and get you first thing tomorrow."

As I spoke I could sense a sort of resignation.

"Arnold is bringing his wife tonight. It's a delicate situation.

It just wouldn't…"

She took my hand and smiled. "It's fine. It's nothing."

I pushed off and rowed for home. I looked back and lined up my marks. She continued to stand on the rocks, looking at me. Her request to come home with me had come out of the blue. It had had just enough urgency to it, that it was disquieting. What had triggered it? I'd been packing up, everything seeming ordinary. She'd been staring off to the north. Had she seen something? I tried to process that, and it sent chills up my back.

Back in the cottage I took a long shower. It had been a lovely day. It seemed like each time our relationship was on the brink of the moment ending, something would inflame it again. How could a beaten up, locked box have led to such a fun and interesting time?

I dressed in nice slacks and a sweater and waited for my brother to arrive. I checked my phone for messages. Just two. One from Graff wondering if I'd made up my mind to take the job; and the other from Angie wondering if some guy had found me. 'I forget to tell you yesterday, but on Wednesday evening just before I closed a man came in and looked at *Passing*. He seemed excited about it and pressed me to introduce him to the artist. I told him to speak with you and told him where you lived. I tell you, John, it's big.' That was the message. I shrugged. No one had tried to contact me yet.

At five on the dot Arnold's car pulled in, crunching across the broken shells. Millions of million dollar shells, I thought. Marsha came in first, looking very proper, but with her face wrinkled — presumably because they'd had to drive through the odors of J&M. The air was fresh here, though, and she smiled her public smile and came close enough for the regulation hug and kiss — a leaning in sort of hug rather than a warm friendly one, and a peck on my unscarred cheek. I find most women prefer to do the kissing that way, rather than let my damaged mouth approach their face. She then stepped back and walked around the room taking it all in, which doesn't take long. Her look was hard to read. Amusement? Curiosity? If she were suspicious about Arnold and another woman, she might have thoughts that they 'did it' here, and she'd be seeking some sign.

Arnold hadn't spoken until she'd finished her inspection and said, "A cute little place you have." Either a compliment or a put down.

Arnold spoke. "I made reservations at Maison Paris," he said. "We should probably head over."

I climbed into the back seat and we drove the ten minutes to the restaurant. I held my breath as we passed Angie's. There in the window was *Passing*. I started to say something, but didn't. Maison Paris is not the five star restaurant that its name might suggest. But it's pretty good; and it is small and quiet. It has a limited menu with a couple of entrees with French names as well as a lot of local sea food.

When Arnold had called in desperation, setting up plans for Friday, he'd said that the worst thing about coming home last

Friday had been that Marsha had just given him 'the look.' She hadn't asked where he'd gone; hadn't asked why he didn't answer his cellphone; didn't ask about what we'd had for dinner. She just looked at him, and said "Freckles is dead," and then walked off to bed. For Arnold, that made the encounter excruciating; but for the two devious, brotherly plotters, cooking up a story, it left the possibilities wide open.

We were seated at a corner table. By this time, simply by watching their manner together, I sensed that the relationship was strained; that it was no longer the happy arc of family that Arnold had described two weeks ago.

"I'm glad you came," I said, lying. "I see so little of you, and we're not that far, after all."

"It's overdue," she replied, professionally. "Arnold tells me a lot about you, of course, and it's nice that you're seeing each other so frequently." Her lip curled up a tad as she'd said "so frequently."

Oh well, it was now or never. Time for the cooked-up story to cover Arnold's disappearance.

"I'm trying to think, Marsha, how long it has actually been since I saw you last. It's too bad that it is things like Freckles dying that lead to a call." Just make everything sound ordinary. "How is Chris taking it?" Keep the focus on the cat.

"He's a little broken up. He used to sleep with Freckles wrapped around his head. He said the purring helped him sleep." Then she slipped in her dagger. "Too bad I couldn't reach Arnold. Chris was right with me when I called. Chris would have liked at that moment to hear something from his father." She was looking straight at me, and not at Arnold at all.

"But Arnold told you, right?" I asked, trying to sound sincere.

"Told me what?"

"Why he left; why you couldn't reach him."

"No," she said. "He didn't. Tell me."

"OK if I tell her?" I asked Arnold.

"I was hoping to keep it secret until Christmas," said Arnold, following his memorized lines.

"What does Christmas have to do with anything," asked Marsha.

"I'm not going to tell you what it is, but Arnold was arranging a Christmas gift for you. He left his phone at my cottage when he ran out, and so never knew you were calling him until the next day. I never heard his phone ring, since I was cleaning up; and frankly it was much later when he came back, noticing he'd forgotten his phone. I was already in bed and neglected to say you'd called."

She stared at me. She either bought it, or decided it was so lame that she'd not bother to follow up. For all I knew, she might already know all about Arnold's affair, and all I was doing was entertaining her.

Whatever the reason, the topic was now closed. She smiled at me and said, "Arnold tells me that you're writing some article about something important in art."

"I am," I said, happy for the change of topic.

We talked about art in general. I told them I had a job offer in Boston, which seemed to immediately elevate me in Marsha's eyes. I asked about Chris and school and whether he'd be getting another cat. We all ate and drank and made it through the evening.

Driving back to the cottage, to drop me off, we again passed Angie's. I don't know why, but I didn't mention the painting. When I was finally alone, I sighed. The evening was over. It was still warm and not too late, so I poured a beer and went outside. The stars were bright and there was only a slight breeze. I looked up at North Egg and could make out the silent woman between the boulders — ever vigilant and watching as if she were some sort of sentry.

I thought about the day with Hester. It had been good. Really good. And it held promise. When I'd taken that first trip to North Egg, I'd been a lost soul, buried in bitterness. At the beginning, our relationship seemed all about me. Through some process, she was showing a new way, a path from bitterness, a way to shed the past and live. It was a moment, and that could have been the end; but it wasn't. We continued to find ways to connect and enjoy. And today convinced me that it might actually be sustainable. That we were finally finding the beginnings of a life that went beyond fragile moments.

CHAPTER Eleven

Beginning

She's not in sight out on the rocks. I go into the house and make a quick tour through the rooms. No sign of her. I glance at the table, remembering the day she'd left a note, "Come back tomorrow," but the table has no note.

I'm in a sort of despair and go back out onto the rocks. An idea strikes me and I walk around the north-east side of the house and over to the fence. Her bike is leaning against it. And that sends a chill up my spine. I walk at a faster pace now around the house, glance at her pile of treasures, and then at the large boulders. I walk along the rocky edges of the point, just looking and searching for any sign of anything.

I finally find her. In a little slit between two rocks on the north edge of the neck, she is lying in the water, for the moment held there by the incoming tide. She is partially submerged, and her caftan softly swirls to and fro with each wavelet; and the rising and receding water creates an illusion that she is breathing. But she is not. She is lying face up, eyes staring, mouth slightly open and filled with water.

Tears well up and I struggle with my bad leg until I'm sitting down on the rock next to her. I see no sign of injury, and I can't help but call up all my mental resources and will her back to life. But I know it won't happen. Tears are running now, down my cheeks, down my scar — the scar she'd touched to tell me it was beautiful.

What happened, Hester? I lean down and look into her dead eyes, staring deeply. She is not a fish, but I am willing the eyes to speak; to tell me a story, a history.

"I asked you to take me with you, yesterday," they say. "It was the one thing I ever asked. Remember when I had glanced to the north. Remember my look? Couldn't you have felt it too? I asked you to take me with you."

Tears are running, and I'm now crying with a voice. So kind and thoughtful a woman. Who could wish her any harm? A small wave crosses her face, and she blinks, her head turning slightly. I see a smile. I look back at the eyes.

"John, remember the stories. It was the best I could do. Our time was so precious and yet so fragile and so important to me. How could I take the risk and give you histories that would destroy it? Stories were the best I could do."

Stories! Suddenly I made another connection, and it made my tears increase. I spoke and said, "Hester, I now know the third thing to take away from the story of Cafka and the Princess."

Her eyes stared back and said, "What is it, John?"

"It is that some stories are unfinished. You didn't finish that one in the telling, and now..." My mind was trying to say, "...our story stays unfinished, and your future is unfinished, and the wonderful art you've created remains unfinished." My mind went on like that, but I was so choked up that I couldn't even speak the words to her.

A wave ran across her lips and she smiled again, but spoke through her eyes. "John, it can also be said that some stories don't end. Isn't that a better thought?"

I looked up. The only sounds were the shore birds and the lapping of the waves. Then there's the sound of a clunk from Osbourne's. Someone is working there. I need to call someone and report this, and I don't carry my cellphone with me in the little boat.

I slowly get up. It's almost impossible to leave her, and I stand there another minute, staring, crying, thinking. Oh Hester. My steps crunch slightly as I walk across broken shells. How could I not take you with me yesterday? You asked, and I let you down. The pain of realizing that I'd turned her down, and had done it for fear that her presence might be embarrassing in front of my brother and family was excruciatingly painful. How could I have been so selfish? It hadn't been a casual request. It was life and death and I'd missed it. The most important person in my life; the most important question she'd asked, and I'd gotten the answer wrong and killed her.

My feet have taken me around the fence and into Osbourne's. The crane operator stops his work and looks down at me.

I can hardly speak. "Do you have a cellphone? Can you call 911"

The man climbed down. "What for?" Gruff, not friendly.

"There's a death. A woman is dead out at the neck."

"Aw, shit! Did she fall in the water? You talking about the old hag?"

I want to hit this man, but I nod. He then looks at me sharply and says, "And who are you? What the fuck are you doing on my property?"

He's leaning into me and I back off. "Relax. Could you just call 911, please?"

"Don't go anywhere," he snarls and dials.

Before the police arrive, we walk back to the neck and talk in an atmosphere of some hostility. I learn that he is Freddie Osbourne, one of the owners of the scrap business. He looks at Hester's body, and nods, now a little softer. "Yeah. That's my aunt. She uses that old house for painting."

"Couldn't she afford an art studio?" I ask.

He looks at me, hostile again. "What are you so nosy about? Why are you here anyway?"

"I was a friend. We sometimes painted together," I said. And that was all I would give up to Freddie, the nephew.

"You think she just fell in? Or what?" he asked me.

I remembered my memories and thoughts as I'd stared into her eyes. "I think she was terrified of someone. I have no idea how she died, but I'm thinking she might have been killed. She's your aunt. What do you think?"

"What I think is none of your fucking business. Shit. Shit." Freddie was staying tough and hostile, but his eyes were wet.

Hours later, when the police dropped me off at my cottage, I was drained of life. I looked out toward the ocean. I walked out onto the rocks and looked north. At North Egg. At the boulders. At my little skiff – still tied up and bobbing gently.

The tape played over and over in my head. "Take me with you."

At the police station Freddie Osbourne and I were interviewed separately. The questions seemed ethereal in some way. I was in shock. The memory of looking into those eyes, the softly shifting caftan; Hester, looking so calm and delicate, gently swirling in the little slit where she lay; the moving water bringing her to life. Almost. Not at all. "Take me with you."

How fitting. The detective's name had been Carp. Detective Carp. I forget his first name if he even told me. I never felt badgered by the questions or that I was a suspect, but nevertheless it was exhausting with long breaks where I was just left alone in a room.

"You said you knew the victim?" Carp asked.

"Victim?" I replied. "So she was killed?"

"It's preliminary at this time, but it appears so. How well did you know her, John?"

"Not well." *Better than I have known most people.* "I've only known her a week or so."

"How did you meet?"

"One day I rowed over to North … to the point behind the scrap pile and she was there."

"Was she expecting you?"

"No. We'd never met before." *I knew you were coming.*

"And so, what? You just talked or what?"

"We talked." *We stood in the doorway naked and then scraped ourselves with oil.* "She's… She was an artist. I write about art. We had something in common."

"How well do you know Freddie Osbourne?"

"Never met him until this morning. Is he a suspect?"

"Why were you there this morning?"

"It was a nice day to row over. We had nothing planned." *I was desperate to see her.*

"Did you touch anything? Take anything from the crime scene?"

"No." *But I looked into your eyes. Oh, Hester.*

Detective Carp left the room. He was gone five or ten minutes. It's hard to tell time when you're alone in an unfamiliar room, hours after you discover someone you love, murdered. Carp returned and we resumed. But it was a strange question.

"John. How well do you know Richard Kommarsch?"

"Who?" I replied. But then something clicked in my mind.

Carp was replying. "Richard Kommarsch. How well do you know him?"

"It took me a second, Detective. There's a moderately well-known artist by that name. But I've never met him."

"You every write to him? Email him? Phone? Any contact?"

"What is this? I know the name. That's it. What does he have to do with this?" I was trying to figure this all out.

"That's what I want to find out. Do you know where he is?" said Carp.

"Detective. I have not heard the man's name or anything about him in decades. He made a splash years ago. That's my entire knowledge of Richard Kommarsch."

"How much time did you spend together with Anne Osbourne?"

"Who is that?"

Carp was good at staying expressionless, but at my reply he looked startled.

"Anne Osbourne. The victim."

"I... I... She told me her name was Hester. That was what she told me."

Carp excused himself again, and I was left to think. I didn't like any of this. Hester was dead. But at least I had me few and fragile memories, and now, Carp and everything else that's going to happen is going to dredge up the life that she had convinced me I didn't need to know. I'd pay a price. And already I was. Anne Osbourne? Of course. Freddie Osbourne's aunt. He'd said it. She was allowed to use that old house as a studio, but I'd never thought... Hester had always carefully closed the curtains in around us. A cocoon of joy and intimacy, not polluted by Freddie Osbourne, or Richard Kommarsch. How could he possibly connect to this? I knew that at this point I didn't want to know. I didn't even want to have heard his name. I wanted to protect my memories as they were.

Carp came back again.

"What we need to do now, John, is to see what you can remember from your visits with Anne that would help us connect this up."

"I'd love to help," I said. "She was a nice and kind woman."

"Did she ever mention Richard Kommarsch?"

"No. And I have no clue as to why you keep mentioning him."

"Well I'm going to tell you, in the hopes that it might help trigger some memory. We're checking all this, but Richard Kommarsch was a well-known artist years ago. You, yourself said you knew the name. Anne Osbourne at that time was his model and maybe his mistress. Kommarsch killed someone — I don't have the details yet. Anne provided testimony that led to his arrest and conviction. He was in prison for 22 years until he was released two years ago."

I'm in shock hearing this, of course. Kommarsch's model and mistress? Murder? Prison? But the chill up my spine is mostly from the last story she told me. Bubble gum. Twenty two pieces to get out of the well. One piece per year. She had been telling me the story of her life.

Carp is looking at me. "You're thinking something?"

"I'm in shock. She never told me anything about her life." I do have to tell him the one thing, though. The one thing in my memory that haunts me. The one thing I should have connected with "Take me with you." It was her look when she stared at something north of the point. A fleeting moment of fear or even terror.

I give it up. "On Friday, we were standing on the rocks. There was a moment when she looked at the shoreline north of the point. She looked so startled and afraid that I actually asked her what it was. I have a feeling she wanted to tell me, but for some reason wouldn't. All she said was "It's nothing. I thought I saw someone.""

"But nothing else?"

"No." Why, Hester, why couldn't you just tell me? You paid a bigger price in the end. *I thought I saw someone.* And then another thought hits me. I thought I saw someone too — not on the north side of North Egg, but next to J&M. Someone I thought was watching for me.

"Do you have any photo of Kommarsch?" I asked.

"Why do you ask?" said Carp.

"I saw someone acting strangely in town. I just wonder…" And the thought terrifies me. Kommarsch a murderer out of prison. Hester had been the instrument of his going to prison for twenty-two years. Had he returned to pay her back? Who else but him. "Take me with you." If only I had. But then the really terrifying thought is that Kommarsch was watching me — if he were to turn out to be the stranger. I saw him Friday as I was setting off for North Egg. Suppose he'd seen where I'd gone. Oh Hester.

But then I am puzzled. If Kommarsch were looking for Hester — Anne — why would he be watching me?

"There's more you want to say?"

"I don't know why I was being spied on, but I was. It's just a strange coincidence, maybe."

"I don't believe in coincidences."

A year passed and it was a week or so after the trial. Kommarsch was locked up, presumably for a long time. After Hester's death, I had thought for long hours about life and meaning and my guilt. I was still fragile, but Hester had awakened something in me that I couldn't lose. Life. Hester had told a story of a princess, ultimately losing her way and drifting through seedy taverns, but ultimately being rescued by a witch, who had given her an incredible gift: Life. Hester had given me the same, and I couldn't lose it. It had been a scary choice to make, but the only one. If I stayed in my cottage and continued to frame pictures and stare at the ocean, I'd fall back into the brooding and bitterness that had held me so long. If I took the job in Boston, I'd be on a new path of possibilities. Terrifying, yet it had to be the right choice. Graff Griffin was willing to take the risk. How could I not?

I drove down from Boston to pick up some paintings of Anne's that had surfaced. I looked at Osborne's and J&M as I drove by. The paintings were at the police station, and while I was there I saw Detective Carp. He waved me over.

"Well, it's all done now," he said. "How are you doing? You were close to her, weren't you. I could tell the trial was hard on you."

"We were closer than you'd think for only knowing her a couple of weeks," I said. In more ways than one. "She was a wonderful woman."

Carp nodded. "I only know her through the record we pieced together. I always had the impression you didn't know much about her background."

"That's true. Nothing," I said. "I still don't know much. The absence of that knowledge was one of the things that, strange as it seems, made her interesting." I hated talking this way about Hester. Every word serving inexorably to reshape my delicate, precious memories into commonalia.

"Well. You cared about her and I thought you might want to hear the whole story." There it was. That magic word, 'story.' Stories had been a spine through our relationship. I thought of Cafka and his brothers; I thought of the dwarf, princesses, bubblegum. But Carp wasn't talking about that sort of story. He was offering up everything that Hester had avoided sharing with me. He was offering context that would reshape and forever change all of my memories. There had been times when I'd been determined to uncover those secrets, and other times — at the moments with her when time and space and place meant nothing and I was glad that the clutter of peripheral knowledge was absent. But now she was dead. *Some stories are never finished.* I had a choice right here to leave this one unfinished; to say to Carp that I didn't want to know, or that I had an appointment and would call him later. Hester, in my shoes, would have found a way to turn the story aside with some sort of kind, caring change of direction. If I said no, I could always change my mind later and hear it then. If I said yes, it would be irreversible.

"John?" Carp said, wondering where I'd gone.

"Part of me doesn't want to hear it. I avoided listening to anything at the trial that I didn't have to hear. I didn't read about it in the papers. But I think I need to now. Tell me."

Carp spoke, and I had a sense he liked telling stories, having created them from puzzle pieces. "Here's what we know:

"Anne Osbourne was born in 1946. The Osbourne family, through two brothers owned Osbourne Scrap & Iron and other related businesses. The family came from a rough background, but Anne's father wanted to move his family in a more genteel direction. The operation of the businesses shifted to the other brother, while Anne's father managed the finances. Her father had visions of Anne as a future socialite and did his best to give her the tools — art lessons, riding lessons, good schools and so on — but he was basically a rough type who, from what we can piece together, forced these things on his daughter rather than offering them.

"University was the first escape for her — the first time she'd had the freedom to make her own choices. This was in the late sixties, and as I'm sure you recall, that was a time when many of the choices students were making were to rebel against convention and get into free sex, drugs, and the like. Hard to tell now, but she was apparently a beautiful girl back then — we have a photo.

"She had been taking art courses at school, but before graduation, left college to run off with a group of hippies. They played around, thought they were the new world; people came and left the group. It was a rough life. They used and sold drugs, although Anne also apparently also sold some small paintings.

"She got pregnant. We have no idea who the father was. As a result, and with a child coming, she moved in with her sister-in-law — that would be Freddie's mother. Anne's own parents wouldn't have her around. They felt their investment in her had gone bad. As far as I know, she never spoke with them again.

"Anne gave birth to a daughter in seventy-two, but after a year moved out, leaving the daughter behind to be raised by Freddie's mother. We can only presume that at this point in her life, Anne must have felt totally alone, embarrassed, helpless, and yet had enough spirit to decide to try to start things anew. As for the daughter, when she found out later that her mother had abandoned her, she refused any contact with her.

"Anne moved in with a woman named Carol Mudders — we don't know how they met. Carol was four years older. She apparently stayed with Mudders for about four or five years and then left to follow a rock band around, selling her pictures at their performances.

"Now here's where it gets interesting and connects up. After about two years of that life, she was noticed by Richard Kommarsch. As I'd said earlier, she was attractive when young. He was a rising painter himself, and wanted a live-in model. This relationship lasted ten years. I've been told that Anne is recognizable in a number of Kommarsch's paintings. During this period, Anne apparently painted too — and we understand from Kommarsch himself that she actually finished a number of his painting for him. He was a heavy drinker and could be nasty when drunk. At one point he broke her nose and knocked out some teeth.

"Anne must have felt increasingly trapped, living with a mean, erratic man. On the other hand, his paintings were selling well and she was probably living better than she had since she'd been a child. In any event, it was presumably a difficult time for her.

"In 1990 she witnessed Kommarsch's murder of another artist. She fled and reported it. He was arrested, tried and convicted. Anne's testimony was the main basis of the conviction. Kommarsch was sent to prison for twenty-two years. Initially, as often happens, the news-value of the murder made his paintings more valuable, and he continued to produce more from prison.

"Later, he slipped from favor and built up an increasing hatred for his ex-model and mistress, Anne, and I'll return to that in a minute, but first we follow Anne. When she fled Kommarsch, she hid various places until he was convicted.

She then moved back in with Carol Mudders. This was about 1994. At that time, Carol's eighty-five-year-old father was in ill health, and Anne helped care for him, presumably in return for room and board, although we know that she also continued to paint and sell paintings.

"She did one other thing. Even though Kommarsch was in prison, she was terrified of him. She changed her name to Janet Forte and tried to stay hidden.

"Mudders' father died in 2004, but Anne — as Janet Forte — continued to live with her, and this continued until 2013, when an unsigned letter arrived for her. We got this from Mudders. The letter simply said, 'Soon, Anne. Soon.' She recognized the handwriting as Kommarsch's. She knew he was at a point where he was coming up for parole review. So she packed her bags and fled. Kommarsch apparently had known about Carol earlier.

"At any rate, when Kommarsch was finally released from prison in 2014, Anne appealed to the family for help. For years she had sent birthday and Christmas cards to her daughter, but had never received a reply. So she appealed to Freddie — the only other close family relative. Freddie helped her find a quiet place to room here in town, and gave her an old bicycle and the use of that old house behind the scrap pile as a studio. He helped her stock it with art supplies and other things, but then, by mutual agreement they didn't meet, since they feared Kommarsch might find her through him.

"Meanwhile, Kommarsch was now free and finding little demand for his art. He set out to follow-up on his threatening note. He contacted Mudders, who told him nothing. He then contacted Anne's daughter, claiming he had some money for her mother. There was no love there, but the daughter had received a birthday card, mailed from here. She told Kommarsch about it.

"He arrived here a week or so before the murder, but couldn't find any sign of Anne — who was still living under the name Janet Forte. He knew that Freddie was her nephew and contacted him. Freddie told him to get lost."

I knew that Carp was now coming to the part of the story I didn't want to hear. The part that involved me and the decisions I made that led to Hester's death. But it was my penance to hear it again.

"And finally we come to the last few days. Kommarsch was about to conclude that Anne had moved on to another town when he happened to see a painting in the window of Angie's Art. That was on Wednesday, late afternoon." *Right. The end of the day I had promised Hester I'd remove the painting, but didn't.*

Carp noticed my expression, but kept going. "Kommarsch was pretty sure he recognized the hand that had painted it and rushed into Angie's to ask how to reach the artist. Ignorant of any risk or threat, Angie told him to contact you, and told him where you lived. He didn't want to actually reveal himself, since at this point he was afraid that whoever you were, you'd be protecting her, so he decided to watch you in the hope that you'd lead him to her.

"He watched your cottage, and when you drove off on Thursday, he thought you'd lead him to his prey, but you drove to Boston, which infuriated him. On Friday morning he watched the cottage again. This time instead of driving somewhere, you left in your skiff. He watched you head off, and then walked down to the shore to keep an eye on where you were heading. You tied up behind Osbourne's.

"Kommarsch could think of no reason why you'd do that unless Anne were there, so he drove up the road, past Osbourne's and parked and secretly made his way to the shoreline. He found a spot where he could watch the point beyond the old house. He observed both of you."

I interrupted. "And Anne saw him, but she didn't tell me."

Carp nodded sympathetically. "After you left, he intended right then to kill her, but thought it best to wait until she left and got her bicycle, which he'd seen leaning on the fence. She never came for the bike. I surmise that, having seen someone she thought was Kommarsch, she decided to remain hidden in the house that night. Kommarsch waited until operations in the scrap yard were done for the day...."

"I don't want to hear any more," I said. "I can surmise the rest, and that's enough."

Being back in town, seeing familiar things, listening to Carp all brought back other memories. After Hester's death, the police had quickly zeroed in on Kommarsch and caught him near the Mexican border. I didn't like Freddie Osbourne, and he didn't like me, but since we were thrown together as sources of testimony, we got to know each other, and a week after Anne Osbourne's funeral — Hester's — I invited him for a coffee.

"What's the deal, John?"

"The deal is Anne's paintings."

"What about them?

"I'm a writer. I write about art, and I'm in the process of writing what I think will be a really important article about a new direction in Fine Art."

"What's that to me?" asked Freddie. "Art isn't my cup of soup."

"But it was Anne's," I said. "Barely a week or so before she died, she began to paint in an entirely new style."

"Good for her," said Freddie, not grasping it at all.

"That new style she created is the subject of my article. Anne actual created something of real importance to the art world."

"No shit. Really?"

"No shit. Do you know Angie Franklin? The owner of Angie's Art?"

"Nope. I've seen her store. Two blocks over, right?"

"Right. Angie and I would like to represent the Osbourne family regarding what happens to Anne's paintings."

"What does that mean. Make it simple."

"It means two things. The paintings are important artistically and historically. They need to be cared for and handled properly. They need to go to the right places. They need to be appraised. Some will end up in museums. Some need to be sold. There is potentially a lot of money in it."

"For that stuff?" he asked, not sure he believed me.

"Yes, for that stuff. I believe that Angie and I can help the family do it right. If it's done wrong, the value is a lot less and Anne's reputation is a lot less."

"What do you get out of it, if I say yes?"

"Thirty percent," I said, staying expressionless. "A lot of what has to be done doesn't generate any money — it's just work on our part."

"That seems like a big cut," said Freddie. "How about fifteen?"

"Freddie, I'm pretty certain that if you were thinking about those paintings at all, you were thinking of them as worth a couple of thousand dollars max. Am I right."

"I hadn't thought about it that much."

"I think, in the end, the seventy percent I'm expecting for the family will be more than a hundred thousand dollars — and maybe a lot more."

"Holy shit." He then looked at me narrowly, studying my scar and lip. "If it is that valuable, how do I know I should let you do it rather than someone else?"

"Because I know more about her art, her style, her significance than anyone else in the world."

He thought for another thirty seconds. "All right, John. You're right. If you hadn't brought it up, I might have even just bulldozed the old house, paintings and all. Deal."

That conversation was the beginning. Angie and I had talked about it almost immediately after Hester's death. When Angie had finally seen a photo of Kommarsch, she confirmed he was the one who had come into the store Wednesday wanting to find the artist. That was painful. If only I'd removed the painting...

I accepted the job with Fine Arts World, but stayed put in the cottage while finishing my big article, and while Angie and I finished negotiations with Freddie. I had a big job ahead of me in Boston. Handling Anne's paintings would also be demanding but would furnish more material for Graff; and Angie could handle most of the leg work. Along with the discovery of dozens of other paintings, word of the undiscovered artist was beginning to leak through the rumor mill. When the appraisals were finished I now estimated everything at seven million. — not counting *Passing*, which I refused to sell.

Carp's history of Anne's life had rattled me. But I had to do one more thing before driving back to Boston. I walked down, past the aroma of J&M and across the broken shells next to the cottage and out onto the rocks. I looked up at North Egg. I stood there a long time, remembering my last trip there, after I'd packed up and was ready to leave the cottage for good.

It was almost a year ago, but such a clear memory. It was the final trip in my skiff, without the sail, rowing across the shallow bay to North Egg and its boulders, just as I'd done that first day. I tied up for the last time at the seawall, giving a quick glance and expecting to see an old woman in a caftan standing there. I hobbled up to the house. It was a hot day as it had been on my first trip there. I kept my clothes on, but stood in the doorway, feeling the breeze and remembering that first time, the air caressing me, standing with Hester, listening to the breeze.

The house was empty. Angie and I had removed all the paintings and supplies. I thought of *Passing*. An embrace across time, and realized that's what I was doing here. The point wasn't empty at all. It was full of talking, laughing, story-telling, discovering a new way to live. It was all still here, just in a different time. I followed Hester around the side of the house to the treasure pile and looked at it with her. No one had touched it. I saw the old Walkman with the Phil Collins cassette, *I don't care anymore*. "I'm learning to care, Hester. I'm learning." I picked it up and put in in my pocket. I saw the metal box, still locked. I picked it up, too. Hester touched my shoulder. "I'm glad you took them," she said. I thought again about the third lesson from a story she'd told. I spoke to her. "Some stories never end."

I took a final look, hobbled to the skiff and rowed away.

THE END

ABOUT THE AUTHOR

Geoffrey Phillips has spent his life writing. Most of his stories explore the present, the future, and the meaning of life.

Phillips lives in Connecticut with his wife and two dogs. He enjoys hiking, gardening, painting, and visiting with his grandchildren.

His books are for young readers are published under the name G.L. Phillips.

Visit him at www.glphillips.com

Made in the USA
Middletown, DE
25 November 2019

79434282R00108